HIS HEALING TOUCH

Autumn Macarthur

ABOUT THE AUTHOR

Autumn Macarthur is a USA Today bestselling author of clean Christian inspirational romances with a strong touch of faith. If you love happy-ever-afters, sweet romance, and Hallmark movies, chances are you'll enjoy her stories!

Originally from Sydney, Australia, she now lives in a small town not far from London, England, with her very English husband (aka The Cat Magnet), and way too many rescue cats for our tiny house! A recent addition to the family are two baby guinea pigs. For such small creatures, they have amazingly huge personalities.

When she's not feeding cats, she hand sews, reads, and most of all writes heartwarming stories of love and faith. With every story, God teaches her the exact same lessons her hero and heroine need to learn to commit to their forever love.

She's also blessed with a chronic health issue that has changed her life in the way it limits her. It hasn't been easy, but she's come to give thanks for the gift hidden in the illness — the way it's taught her patience, brought her into a greater dependence on God, and given her a far deeper appreciation of His love and provision.

You can visit her at her website http://faithhopeandheartwarming.com, on Facebook as Autumn Macarthur, and on Twitter as @autumnmacarthur. She'd love to hear from you!

Faith, hope, & heartwarming —
Real romance, real faith.
Inspirational romance to make you smile.

His Healing Touch

Sweetapple Falls #2

Have I not commanded you?
Be strong and courageous.
Do not be afraid; do not be discouraged,
for the Lord your God will be with you
wherever you go.

Joshua 1:9 (NIV)

AUTUMN MACARTHUR

DEAR READER

Have you ever suffered such a huge loss or challenge that it rocked not just your life but your faith in God? Adam and Lainie, the hero and heroine of this book certainly have, and I admit, I have too!

I spent way too many years caught up in the wilderness of resentment and grief, blinding me to God's love and all that was good in my life. Terrible things can and do happen in this world, and often it takes time to see the good God always brings from them.

Adam and Lainie find their way through to love and renewed faith, thanks to the support of the Sweetapple Falls residents and God's determination to woo us back to Him, but it's not an easy journey for them.

Like I did, they rediscover trust in God's goodness and love, and can believe again that He does have a loving plan and purpose for every single one of us. If you're struggling with any difficulty in your life right now, my prayer is that you will discover that, too, will feel God's loving support.

I hope you enjoy Lainie and Adam's story, and that it blesses and uplifts you.

CHAPTER ONE

LAINIE SULLIVAN NUDGED the throttle of her dad's 1985 Honda Goldwing further open as she passed the sign announcing she could finally hit sixty-five. A straight stretch of highway, good weather, little traffic. A chance to make up time after a winding section with a lower speed limit. Beautiful to travel through, but slower riding.

As soon as the bike went over sixty, the engine sound altered. A noise she couldn't identify but probably didn't mean anything good. She grimaced and eased back to fifty-five.

Ugh. The bike still felt way less responsive than she liked, too. It couldn't be the micro trailer she towed, as the last mechanic she took the bike to claimed. He'd treated her like a silly girl with no idea about engines.

The trailer hadn't changed. Yet the engine note had.

Plus, last time she bought gas she'd needed to top up the oil as well, sooner than expected.

Time to stop telling herself everything would be fine. Five hours out of Portland on Interstate 5, smack in the middle of Nowheresville, Oregon, was *not* the place for engine trouble.

Maybe putting as many miles as she had on the bike these past few months wasn't a wise idea, after all. Pushing on, in the hope the patronizing mechanic was right, that she'd imagined it or it wasn't serious or it would go away — definitely not so wise.

Next town she came to, she'd consider stopping.

After too many miles and still no town, she was almost ready to turn around and go back, no matter how much time it lost. The sign inviting travelers to exit the highway in a mile and visit historic Sweetapple Falls couldn't be better timed.

Though rather than apples, the sign showed old-timey storefronts along with a hot-air balloon floating above a vineyard and a cherry orchard. The mismatch tickled her memory.

A patient she'd nursed, one of the many wounded warriors in the military hospital in Maryland. Brown hair, sun-bleached at the tips. A grin with enough sunshine to brighten the dullest day. Dark eyes stubbornly staring at the ceiling to avoid glancing at the shattered wreckage of his leg. A once-tanned face, gray and tight with the pain his wound care caused. Single-minded determination to save his leg, regain his fitness, and get back to active duty. Faith that God would make it possible.

Adam something?

As she'd worked on his many wounds, he spoke often of his Oregon hometown. His family. The local football team. The delicious homegrown pears and cherries. The balloon ride he'd treated one of his sisters to for her birthday.

He'd talked to himself as much as her, something safer to focus on than his injuries. Only the strain in his voice and the absence of his usual grin betrayed how much the dressing changes hurt. When pain dried up his words, she'd babbled herself.

Her plans for her wedding to Michael, a hospital administrator who attended her church. Dad's plans to ride his classic bike right around the country as a cancer fundraiser when he retired. Sports results. Anything she could think of.

She'd prayed for all her patients back then, but Adam inspired extra prayer. An Army medic, he understood more than most just how severe his injuries were. Yet he stayed positive and never once complained, his hope, courage, and faith inspiring her.

Then she left to care for Dad, exchanging a full list of patients for just one. She never did discover what happened to most of the warriors she'd nursed for so long.

Maybe this visit to his hometown would tell her. Even without the odd engine noise, she would've wanted to detour when she saw the sign. Though, so late in December, she really should be moving south, not planning a detour.

Nearing the junction, she flicked on the turn indicator.

Forget former patients for now. The bike *did* have the engine noise. If she found out about Adam, that was a bonus. Locating a well-equipped workshop with a mechanic who understood older motorcycles had to be her priority.

Finding what she needed in a small rural town might be the problem. Tractors and pickups, sure. Vintage bikes in need of TLC, maybe not. If this town had the right sort of workshop, she might even stay overnight.

At the town limits, a sign advertising the Christmas Lights Trail welcomed her.

Just a few blocks on, past a scattering of newer homes and a few fine old Victorians, all draped with lights and holiday decorations, she spotted it. An old-style, flat-fronted gas station with a more modern three-bay workshop beside it. Hard to miss, as it carried twice as many lights as the neighboring homes combined. Still, the place beckoned her in.

Sweetapple Falls Automotive. Perfect.

She just had to hope the proprietors knew as much about motorcycles as they appeared to know about setting up Christmas displays. An entire nativity scene in lights filled the front of the building. This town sure took their seasonal displays seriously.

At her first glance around the workshop interior, the huge piece of farm machinery occupying the middle bay didn't reassure, though the orderly array of tools in their marked slots on the pegboarded back wall showed attention to detail.

Then she spotted the vintage Buell in a corner. Covered with a light coating of dust, as if it hadn't been worked on for a while. But surely, someone here must understand bikes. Her tight shoulders relaxed. If she still believed God heard her prayers, she'd be thanking Him right now.

After riding up to the door marked Office, she stopped, clambered off the big bike, dropped the stand into place, and then lifted her helmet visor. Bing Crosby crooning "White Christmas" welcomed her. She hoped that wasn't prophetic. A white Christmas was the last thing she wanted.

Leaving the monster yellow machine, a fortyish guy, his dark hair sprinkled with gray, wiped dirty hands on the rag sticking out of his coveralls and sauntered toward her.

"Tom Davis, ma'am. How can I help you?" He nodded respectfully at the bike and the small enclosed trailer it towed. "Nice rig."

"Thank you." She smiled. His welcome and respect was balm to her soul after that last mechanic.

Davis. Wasn't that the last name of her patient? A brother? But she'd met Adam's mom and his sisters during her time caring for him. Surely a brother would have visited, too. In small towns, the same names cropped up again and again. Go back far enough, and almost everyone was related.

With an effort, she dragged her thoughts away from the patient she'd grown far too attached to and focused on why she'd stopped here.

"I'm concerned the bike may not be running as nice as it looks. The engine feels a little off, and it's using more oil than usual. I have to cover a lot of miles to get south before winter closes in. I need to know if I'm safe to continue."

Dad would have known instantly what the problem was, of course.

The grief she should be way more accustomed to twisted her heart, as it did every time she thought of him. His death left a gaping hole in her life and a nagging sense of failure. All her nursing care and all her prayers and all her tears hadn't changed anything.

This man didn't need to know any of that. But keeping her friendly smile pinned in place became a whole lot harder.

The mechanic spread his oil-stained hands wide. "Ma'am, I'm happy to take a look at it, but I'll be honest with you. Working on these machines isn't something I claim to be skilled at."

She gestured toward the Buell. "Who looks after that one?"

His lips turned down as he glanced at the bike. "It's my cousin's. He knows plenty about motorcycles, but it's a while since he was in here last."

His cousin could be her patient. She itched to ask how he was, but didn't. Chasing news of a patient wasn't a good enough reason to spend any longer here. The early-morning chill and the frost coating her bike when she'd begun today's ride not long after dawn warned her not to linger.

Yet still, she hesitated. Once she hit Northern California, she'd face a long empty stretch with no towns. And because the ride progressed slower than she hoped today, she didn't have enough daylight left to reach Sacramento.

"No one in town can check my bike for me? I really need to know if I'm safe to ride on. Your cousin would be better than nothing."

Tom's face scrunched. "I'm not sure he'd come look at it. He's going through a tough time right now." Doubt further creased his brow. "I guess I can ask if he's able to drop by. But he's not qualified. I can't guarantee his work."

The guy didn't sound encouraging.

"Please ask. If he's happy to do it and you're happy to let him, then I'm happy, too." Wanting to see Adam again, if he really was the mechanic's cousin, had nothing to do with her choice.

"I'll give him a call. He might come. He might not."

The mechanic dialed and then shouted into his cellphone for a minute. "Great! Adam's agreed to come and look. Do him good to get out of the house." Sadness shadowed his eyes. "Army vet, he's still not walking too well. He lives close by, but it could take him fifteen minutes."

The Adam she remembered. Had to be. Though till she saw him, she couldn't be sure.

What she *could* be sure of was the need to stomp hard on the odd little jump her heart made. Being so glad to see a patient again was less than ethical or professional.

She wanted the best for every patient, of course, and felt a proper concern for them. But she'd felt more than she should for him. If not for being able to remind herself of her engagement to Michael, the only option would have been to ask another wound care nurse to treat Adam.

Perhaps she should have, anyway.

As she cared for his terrible injuries, she'd chattered about her wedding plans. He'd talked to distract himself from his wounds and his pain. She'd talked to distract herself from *him*.

Now, she had no engagement to hide behind. Just a need to keep moving.

And the mechanic's sadness suggested Adam's recovery hadn't worked out as he'd hoped, even after almost a year. With injuries so severe, chances were he might never fully recover.

"You can take a seat over there if you want." Tom waved toward an old office chair in one corner, beside a scrawny tinsel-draped fake Christmas tree. Looked like the Christmas spirit extended only to the lighting and the sound system. "And help yourself to a soda from the fridge."

"Thanks." She pulled her Kindle and a water bottle from her tank bag and sat to read while waiting.

A couple of chapters into her cozy mystery, Tom's voice echoed through the workshop. "Adam, good to see you!"

Her breath caught in her throat as she glanced across to the open workshop entrance.

It *was* the Adam she'd nursed, leaning on a pair of forearm crutches.

He'd bulked up in his upper body compared to when she last saw him, probably done weights to build back the muscle mass his extended immobility chewed away. But his skin retained its hospital pallor. His hair had darkened, like a man who didn't get outdoors much. He hadn't shaved for a couple of days.

Could be intentional. Designer stubble. But Adam's listless downcast eyes betrayed his mental state.

The eyes of a man who'd lost hope. What had happened to the determined faith she'd admired? Dad's eyes dulled the same way near the end, when he'd known the cancer beat him.

"Is this the bike you want me to look at, cuz?" Desolation flattened Adam's voice.

Though perhaps he'd superficially recovered, he didn't look or sound good. Not good at all.

Tom waved toward her. "Lady needs someone to look at her machine. I told her you're the motorcycle expert around here. Willing to give it a once-over?" His overly cheerful voice, louder than necessary, signaled Adam still had some blast-induced hearing damage.

Adam glanced at the bike, not her, then nodded.

Unless he said something, she wouldn't mention knowing him. No reason he should recognize her. Just because she'd seen him as a special patient didn't mean he'd remember her as any more than one of many nurses in and out of his room during his months in the hospital.

When he stepped toward the bike, she realized what stole his hope. Why he showed little trace of the spirit she'd thought as much a part of him as his brown eyes.

No surprise he still needed crutches with a leg as shattered as his had been. But the way he flung his left foot forward and an unmistakable hitch in his gait told her. Almost certainly, the left leg had required amputation. And worse, above the knee.

Compassion stopped her breath and twisted a hard, painful knot in her chest.

Gone. The leg she and the rest of the surgical team had worked so hard to save. The leg he'd endured so much to keep.

Adjusting to the effects of his injuries and life without his military career wouldn't come easy to a man like Adam. Angry tears burned her eyelids.

Life was unfair. *God* was unfair. When He could heal people, why didn't He?

A small silver cross, the one Adam's mom had dangled from his hospital bed in the ICU then clipped around his neck as soon as he came off life support, still gleamed at his neck.

Didn't God help His people anymore?

Pointless question. God didn't answer her now, any more than He had when Dad's condition worsened.

Just like Dad, Adam had fought and fought and fought.

And just like Dad, he'd lost in the end.

"You okay?" Tom asked, brow creased in concern as he gazed at Adam. "I'm guessing the walk here's the longest you've done since getting home."

"Yep." He swayed where he stood. Clearly, his answer referred to the walk, not how he was. Not exactly okay, there.

Tom grabbed the chair she'd sat on. "If you need to sit and rest, I've got a chair here for you."

Adam shook his head. "I can do it. I'm fine." Strain hoarsened his voice, and he moved slower as he approached the bike.

He wasn't fine, but Tom didn't argue. With a resigned sigh, he rolled the chair nearer so Adam had the option to sit while he checked the bike.

The workshop became far too hot. Stifling. She unzipped her leather jacket and swept her hair off her face, resisting the urge to run her fingers through it. As if it mattered what she looked like. Adam had more important things to think about.

Things like staying upright and taking a few more steps.

But irrelevant as it was, she still *did* wish her hair looked nicer. All those movie scenes where the girl pulls off her helmet and her beautiful hair bounces down? Reality bore no resemblance. The helmet flattened everything it covered, and the wind tangled the rest. Little remained of the neat braid she'd started the day with.

Bitterness twisting his lips, Adam lowered himself into the chair Tom held for him. As his shoulders slumped, he blew out a breath.

"Thanks for being willing to check my bike." She stepped forward.

He glanced up. Recognition sparked his eyes, but he didn't smile. "Lainie. What are you doing here?"

So he wasn't happy to see her.

No matter. Her feelings for him had to be clamped down tight, as much now as when he'd been her patient. Changing out of her scrubs didn't make her any less a nurse.

Besides, Adam still needed care. Seeing her patient with spirits as shattered as his leg broke something in her. She didn't know how, but she ached to help him regain his lost hope.

For the first time in months, she prayed.

Will You show me how to help Adam, Lord? Please?

CHAPTER TWO

LAINIE, HERE in Sweetapple Falls, riding a motorbike? Adam's chest tightened. Great to see his favorite nurse again, sure. But last he knew, she'd been about to get married.

Most of the staff were caring, conscientious, efficient. She'd been all that and more. When Lainie worked on his leg, he'd felt she saw *him*. A person, not a messy list of medical problems.

If she hadn't been engaged, if he hadn't been a smashed-up wreck, he would've asked her on a date once he escaped the hospital. There'd be a line to wait in, for sure. Him and most of her male patients.

A woman like her was easy to fall in love with, and he'd had nine long weeks to do it.

Seeing Lainie again snagged at his heart, reminding him of all he'd lost. More than just his leg. Back when she'd nursed him, he still had hope, and he still had faith. When the surgeon told him he'd die if he didn't consent to the amputation, he'd lost them, too.

Since they cut off his leg, he was hollow and empty. A nothing, a zero, zilch. No leg. No job. No life. People told him he was lucky to be alive, but they had no idea. Maybe the buddies he'd failed to help after the IED blew their vehicle apart were the lucky ones.

As if coming to the Automotive and seeing the Buell he could no longer ride wasn't tough enough, it had to be Lainie's bike Tom asked him to check over.

"So you two know each other?" Tom stated the obvious.

Lainie nodded. "I was a nurse at the military hospital." As she spoke, she gazed at him, not Tom. Assessing if she'd pitched her voice right? A nurse like Lainie would remember the blast also damaged his hearing.

Adam heard every word she said. He bet she'd guessed about his leg, too, but chose to say nothing. Most people weren't nearly so perceptive. And once they knew, they made far more of an issue of it.

In this, as in most other things, Lainie was different.

"Adam, you okay if I get on with the repairs to Jim Mitchell's machine or will you need my help? I can get the bike up on the stand for you."

He suppressed a cringe, the words scraping down his spine like nails on a blackboard. Tom meant well. He should be thankful people in this town cared. Some guys didn't have the support he had. Still, he could do without constant fussing.

"I'm fine. I can manage." The reflex words shot out.

Accepting people's help shrunk him down to kid-sized. Like the ten-year-old he'd been when he first started hanging around Uncle Frank's workshop after Dad died.

Maybe a kid like Josh, born disabled, was used to it. He'd never be.

As Tom headed to the harvester, Adam couldn't help staring at Lainie. So lovely in form-fitting jeans and a greeny-blue T-shirt peeking out from under a leather jacket, her honey-blonde wind-tangled hair streaming down her back.

He'd often wondered what she looked like wearing something other than regulation scrubs.

Now he knew.

Even more beautiful than he remembered. Something he hadn't felt in the longest time sparked. Something he shouldn't be feeling for a married woman.

Not that his feelings for Lainie had been any more appropriate for an engaged woman.

Especially one who was his nurse.

"What brings you here?" Repeating his question seemed safer than voicing his real thoughts — *What happened to your wedding plans, and wasn't it your dad who planned to make the epic bike tour?*

Those questions overstepped the invisible boundary line between nurse and patient. She'd always been careful to go only so far in her friendly chatter and no further. Anything more personal was out of bounds, and he'd instinctively recognized and respected it.

You're not her patient anymore. We're just two people talking about motorcycles.

Right. But he still wouldn't ask. She'd tell him if she wanted to. For her to be here, things must have gone wrong with both her wedding plans and her dad. Possibly in ways that hurt to talk about. He'd had plenty of practice being on the receiving end of that.

That didn't stop him from glancing at her left hand. No wedding ring.

Still single.

That changed nothing. Didn't make him a catch for a girl like her. No leg. No job. Unable to walk a single block. Living in a backyard apartment at his mom's. He'd be better off forgetting he'd ever had feelings for *any* woman, married or single.

Lainie gave him a tentative smile, as if uncertain how much to say. "I'm headed for California. When I noticed the bike didn't feel right, I decided not to keep riding and risk breaking down miles from anywhere."

Not really an answer for why she was in Oregon and in Sweetapple Falls, of all places, when her hometown was in Maryland.

But he had no right to ask. Focus on the bike.

"What's the problem?" He waved at the gleaming classic beauty she rode.

"It feels more sluggish than it did when I started this trip, and I'm sure I've seen it blow blue smoke a couple of times. It's using more oil, too." She spread her hands and shrugged. "This was Dad's bike, and I used to help him work on it. He told me blue smoke was a bad sign. I had it checked out by a mechanic a week back who didn't find anything. Today, my gut feeling told me to stop and get it checked again. I'm just not happy with the way it's running. Especially when I need to cover a lot more miles."

Instead of using his good leg to scoot the chair nearer to the bike and take a look, he simply listened. He'd never forget her expressive voice.

Their long conversations while she'd tended his wounds, apologetic for the pain she caused, cheerfully chattering as she worked. She'd tried so hard to keep his mind off what she was doing, and he appreciated it. The other nurses and the doctors insisted on giving a step-by-step description of what they were doing.

The last thing he'd needed.

Lainie was the only one who'd realized he wasn't in denial. He knew the blast smashed him up almost as bad as his dead buddies. He simply hadn't wanted to be punched in the face with it.

"After you stopped coming to do my leg, I missed you." Why had he blurted that out? It was the truth, but she didn't need to know.

Her soft pink lips curved downward, and his gut twisted as sadness shadowed her blue eyes, leaving no trace of their sparkle.

"I'm sorry I didn't say goodbye. I didn't have the chance to, not with anyone. I got a call from home and had to leave town urgently." Both hands rose to cover her crumpling face. When she lowered them, her usual composure masked her features, but pain lingered in her darkened eyes. "My father suddenly fell ill. By the time he saw the doctor, the cancer had already spread. He needed to start treatment straight away. I left the hospital to care for him."

Shoulders tensed by this glimpse of her heartache, he nodded.

Lainie waved at the banners on the side of the bike trailer. "Mom was a nurse, too, but she died of cancer when I was fifteen. I'm sure I mentioned that doing this fundraiser in her memory was Dad's retirement dream?"

"Yep. So you're doing it for him?" He softened his voice, guessing the outcome. If her dad got well, Lainie wouldn't be doing a 'round-America ride for The Elaine Sullivan Cancer Nursing Fund.

Lips thinned, eyes bright with tears, Lainie shrugged. "He died."

The two words held a universe of grief. When his dad died in a car crash, it tore him up inside. Knowing he shouldn't, he reached a hand toward her anyway. "I'm sorry."

She stepped back, sweeping her unruly hair over her shoulders. "It was months ago. It will get easier. I'm fine. Truly." Her fingers massaged her forehead, hiding her face again.

"Are you?" A short, sharp bark that might have been a laugh escaped him. "I'm the king of 'I'm fine', so I know what those two words really mean. I almost ordered a T-shirt with it printed on the front. Save me saying it twenty times a day."

"When you order it, get one for me, too." Her smile held no more happiness than his laugh had. "Okay, the truth is, I miss him terribly. I have no family left now. But any sympathy makes me cry."

He got that. Not that he'd ever cried, but he hated pity and sympathy.

When he came home, he'd had plenty enough of it. Everyone wanted to tell him how terrible what happened to him was. Like he didn't know? And worst of all was the unwanted advice.

Getting through that had been almost as tough as getting through the first weeks after the amputation.

Seeing the grief Mom tried to hide still was.

Lainie forced a chuckle. "I'm sure you're wondering what happened to my fiancé, too."

He lifted one shoulder and spread his hands. "It's none of my business, but you talked a lot about your wedding plans."

"Turned out I had a narrow escape. I wanted —"

"Everything okay, Adam?" Tom's shout interrupted whatever Lainie started to say.

Adam smiled and gave a thumbs-up. "Just catching up before I look at the bike. We're fine."

His gaze and Lainie's met. As soon as Tom turned back to the harvester and couldn't see them, he rolled his eyes. This time, her chuckle at their shared joke was for real. Her mobile lips quirked in mock disapproval.

"You were saying?" He could listen to her sweet tones all day.

"I wanted to delay the wedding so I could focus on helping Dad through his cancer journey." She shook her head, tears glistening in her lovely eyes. "His oncologist was upfront with us — it might not last long and it might not end well. But when I asked Michael to change the date, he told me I'd better be careful."

"Careful of what?" Adam's brow creased.

"Him finding someone else. I told you Michael's disabled?"

Adam nodded. "I recall you mentioning the search you had locating a reception place accessible for his wheelchair."

"Right. And when he heard I needed to delay our plans, it turned into an argument. He told me he only wanted to marry a nurse so he had someone to look after him who'd be too guilty to ever leave him. According to him, all nurses want someone to care for, and that made us suckers for a guy in a wheelchair." She loosed an eyeroll of her own. "So if I insisted on staying home with Dad, he'd find someone else. Any nurse would do."

An edge he'd never heard in her usually gentle and cheerful voice sharpened her words.

His fists clenched. How could any man who could have married Lainie think for one minute that "any nurse would do"?

Lainie snorted. "Turned out I wasn't such a sucker as he thought. I suggested if that was what he wanted, I wished him well. He more or less kept to the wedding arrangements we'd made, just switched out the bride for a nurse from the cardiac unit." Her gaze dropped. "Sorry, TMI. You probably guessed I'm still pretty bitter about it. I can't believe I fell for him."

"The guy's a…" He caught back the swear word he'd almost let fly. "A fool."

"And whatever you didn't say, too." Her demure tone contradicted the mischief dancing in her eyes.

For the first time since losing his leg, he laughed. A real, honest-to-goodness, that's-so-funny laugh. He had to hold back words even less appropriate than the cuss. *I love you, Lainie Sullivan.*

He thought he did when she'd nursed him, and seeing her again confirmed it. For all he'd tried to tell himself that everyone fell in love with their nurses, there'd been something special about Lainie. After she stopped coming to do his wound care, he did his best to forget her. He'd had plenty else to think about.

All it took was one glance to remind him just how far from forgotten she was.

But her plans surely didn't include getting tangled with another disabled guy. If they did, he'd have to wonder if her fool of an ex was right. Some professional helpers craved victims to rescue 24/7, not only when they were on duty. He'd seen that unhealthy trait in other Army medics.

Was Lainie the same?

Despite what that bomb did to him, he was no victim. He didn't need any nurse, not even Lainie, wanting to look after him. He got enough of that from his family.

"Let's see if there's anything wrong enough with the bike to prevent you from moving on. I'm sure you want to get back on the road again." His voice rasped. Seeing her go would tear him apart, so the sooner it happened, the better. "Can you manage to push it over to the corner? I've got it set up for working on bikes."

As he gestured toward his abandoned bike, his stomach roiled.

He should've asked Tom to sell the thing before he came home.

No point keeping it when the most he could do was to polish it now and then. He hadn't done even that. He'd never be able to ride again. Not with the balance problems the blast wave concussion left him with. Besides, staying upright on two wheels needed two legs.

Not one, and a lifeless chunk of metal and plastic.

Face it, Davis, you're a wreck.

In the hospital, he'd needed Lainie. Not just her gentle touch and her expertise as she'd worked on his wounds. Her sunny smile made hope for recovery seem possible.

But now? He had no hope.

He didn't want to need anyone. And he had nothing to offer a woman.

Especially a woman like her.

CHAPTER THREE

LAINIE'S HEART ACHED for Adam. Impossible to miss the grief in his gaze when he looked at his bike.

You'll ride again. She bit her lower lip to hold back the false reassurance.

How could she be sure?

Plenty of amputees could, but most amps were below the knee, not above. And most amputees hadn't survived the horrific combination of trauma he had. Weeks on life support in ICU, unable to breathe on his own. Traumatic brain injury. Chest drains. Multiple surgeries for internal injuries and ruptured eardrums. And then all the surgeries aiming to salvage his leg.

If Adam's rehab team suggested any possibility he might ride again, surely he wouldn't look so hopeless.

His lip curled as if he guessed her thoughts. "I ought to sell it. Haven't been able to bring myself to do it yet."

"I can imagine it's not easy." She nodded slowly, unsure whether to share her own experience when it didn't compare to what Adam had endured. Donating Dad's clothes to charity and clearing the house ready to rent out while she traveled broke her heart.

Every time she let something of his go, another piece of him died to her.

Reason to cling to Dad's beloved bike and the trip he'd dreamed of all the more fiercely. She grasped the handlebars, as much to feel a sense of connection to her father as to move the big sucker forward.

Not surprising Adam also clung to remnants of his old life.

"Can you manage?" Adam moved to help, then stopped, blowing a frustrated breath through clenched teeth. Rolling his eyes heavenward, he shook his head. "I can't believe I *still* forget. I'll call Tom over."

She lifted a hand to stop him. "No need. Dad installed an electric center stand. I should unhitch the trailer first so I'm not moving its weight too, but that's no problem. I've had plenty of practice. I'm fine."

Emphasizing the last word, she peeped at him under her lashes. Would he recognize the joke?

His twisted lips showed he had. "We really *do* need those T-shirts. Okay, let's see you work this magic." He left his crutches on the floor and scooted on the wheeled chair to the back of the bike.

After lowering the trailer support, she unhitched it deftly and then smiled at Adam. "See, no magic there."

"Does it slow the bike down?" Interest sparked in his voice. "I've never seen a bike towing anything like it before."

"As long as the bike's engine is big enough, it shouldn't slow things by much. I wish I didn't need it, but I aim to book at least one speaking engagement in every town I visit, to help with the fundraising. That calls for fancier clothes and shoes. Can't fit it all in the top box or the panniers." Chuckling, she tapped the storage compartment on the back of the bike. Big enough to hold a full-face helmet and not a lot else. "My friends tell me, when they go on vacation, they take bigger luggage just for their makeup."

"I'm guessing you don't need to."

The appreciation glowing in his dark gaze warmed her far more than it should. Michael never once made her feel so — she struggled for the right word — so entirely *womanly*. Not appropriate feelings for a patient to stir in her.

Especially when she had to move on as soon as she could.

She had a lot more of the country to cover before she completed what she'd set out to do. Achieve the dream his cancer stopped Dad from achieving. The trip he'd planned as a memorial for Mom became a memorial for both of them. Before he died, she promised him she'd do it.

No need to explain any of that to Adam. Instead, she raised her hands to mime a small purse. "Mine fits in that. Okay, now I'll prove I can move the bike."

She waited for Adam to scoot along beside her before switching the bike's ignition on and activating the electric center stand. Once it lowered the bike, she steadied the heavy machine and pushed forward. The bike rolled easily, but she took it slowly.

"You can stop right there," Adam said.

Bracing the bike against her hip, she hit the control switch again to activate the stand. Hard to restrain a smile at the respect in Adam's approving nod.

Almost as hard not to suggest he could get one for his bike, as well.

Too like the well-meaning comments she'd fielded when Dad was ill. How he'd recover if only he took the right vitamins or used the right essential oils or prayed more.

Oversimplifying something so complicated with a "why don't you?" bordered on hurtful.

If Adam thought an electric stand would make a difference, he'd get one.

"Clever." He nodded again, this time toward the bike, not her.

"It's a huge help. As long as I don't let the bike start leaning, I'm okay." Shrugging, she laughed. "Of course, if it tips and I drop it, I have no idea how I'd ever get it upright again."

Adam quirked an eyebrow. "I guess if you drop it, that's the time to stop saying you're fine."

A chuckle escaped her. "Guess so. Gotta happen sometime for us all."

His expression hardened. "Not necessarily *all* of us."

Oops. Turning back to the bike, she pretended they'd been talking about it all along. "So I'll make sure not to tip it over. What next? You want me to start it up?" Her voice rang hollow and fake. Far too chirpy.

Thankfully, Adam didn't notice. Or, more likely, he *had* but chose to ignore it. "Not yet. It's easier for me to check if I hoist it. Just let me look at this." He reached under his office chair and dropped it to its lowest level, then bent almost double to examine the center stand mechanism. "Okay, I think we can use the hoist without damaging anything. Would you drag that blue contraption over, please?"

On wheels, the hydraulic lift took little effort for her to move into place. "Dad had the same one. I hated letting his tools go as part of the estate sale."

"Are you okay with me using it? I can figure out another way if it brings back sad memories." The concern in his questioning gaze touched her.

She smiled. "No need. It's comforting. Kind of nostalgic."

It was. Instead of overwhelming her with grief as she'd expected, the familiarity of many of the tools in this corner of the workshop felt like coming home.

So did working with Adam.

They slipped into an easy pattern. Teamwork. Like with Dad or her favorite surgeons at the hospital. They worked well together.

She helped raise the bike off the ground on the hoist, answered the questions he asked about its service history, and then did what he requested while he scooted his chair around assessing the bike. Started the engine, opened up the throttle, fetched tools, laid any parts he removed to one side where they wouldn't get lost or damaged.

And worried what his deepening frown meant.

Finally, she had to ask. "What do you think the problem is?"

He grimaced and shook his head a little. "You're not going to like it. With the number of miles it has on it, I think the bike may need a full engine rebuild. At least, it needs the valves and the cylinder heads remachined. The problem there's why you've noticed the bike losing both power and oil."

"I'm guessing it's not going to be a quick easy fix. Or cheap." Hands clasped in front of her chest, holding her breath, she studied Adam and waited for his reply.

Please say otherwise.

"Sorry. It's not." He lifted his hands in apology. "When my bike needed similar work, it took two weeks. Probably three for this one, over the holidays. And though the guys I sent my engine to for a rebuild priced their work fairly, it still added up."

She didn't doubt Adam was correct. The confident and systematic way he'd examined the bike showed he approached his diagnostic process as systematically as a good doctor. Far more so than that mechanic back home or the one in Minnesota. But she couldn't really afford two or three weeks with the bike out of action. Or expensive repairs, either.

"Does this need doing straight away? Could I keep going and only get it done when it *really* needs doing?" She didn't quite manage to restrain a worried frown, and bit on a thumbnail. "I want to get far enough south not to have to ride in snow. Being stuck in one place till after Christmas isn't part of my plan. Especially with more wintry weather on its way."

And especially when being stuck here meant being stuck with Adam. The only way to deal with her inappropriate feelings for him was to leave, ASAP.

"Impossible to say. It could last out for two thousand miles or two. But I doubt you'll get through many more states without getting it done. You'll need to take it easy for a while after the work, too, till it's run in."

She loosed a long frustrated breath. Something like this could demolish all her fundraising plans.

As if he guessed her thoughts, Adam raised his shoulders and spread his hands in apology. "I'm not a mechanic. You could wait till you reach a bigger town with a dedicated motorcycle workshop for an expert opinion. I'll get it rideable again so you can decide."

"Where's the nearest one?"

"A good one who can deal with a bike like this?" Adam grimaced. "If you're willing to ride back the way you came, Eugene. If you want to keep moving south, probably not till Sacramento. That's where I sent my bike engine."

As she passed him parts and tools to reassemble everything he'd removed, she wrestled with the problem. Going back wasn't a good option. She needed to keep moving forward. But opting for the long ride to Sacramento didn't feel too wise, either. Even if she could get there before dark, breaking down in the middle of nowhere featured in her nightmares. She didn't want to risk it in real life.

Then there was the cost to consider. Having to dip into her emergency fund so early in the trip bothered her. She thought she'd planned so carefully.

Obviously, not carefully enough.

"I need to work out how much of my budget three weeks at the motel would chew up, on top of the repairs." Rubbing her nose, she multiplied the room rate she'd seen as she rode past by twenty nights and came up with a scarily big number. "Is there any lower-priced accommodation in town? A bed and breakfast?"

"Nothing like that, sorry. I think the Tanners are starting one before next tourist season, but Luke's still working on their house."

Her heart dropped to the soles of her motorcycle boots. Way less expensive than a city, of course, but more than she could easily afford for three weeks getting nowhere. And she still had to pay for the repairs. "Any idea how much the repairs will be?"

He pulled his cellphone from a pocket. "I'll check online for the workshop I used. See if they give a ballpark estimate for the engine rebuild. When I checked around before, they offered the best deal."

The figure he named was lower than she'd expected. Chewing on a knuckle, she did the math. "I could afford that and the motel. Just. But if I pay your guys for a rebuild, then I need to pay someone else to take the engine out and put it back in again, right?"

Smiling, Adam shook his head. "Wrong. Or not here, anyway. I won't charge for my labor, and I doubt Tom will want anything for the use of his workshop, either. He's a good guy. Call it a contribution to your charity if it makes you feel better."

She blew out a slow thoughtful breath and rubbed her forehead. "If it's a donation, I can give you and Tom receipts for your time and labor to claim on taxes. Sounds like I'm going to have to get it done here. I can't risk breaking down on the road, and I'm guessing it will cost a lot more somewhere else. That would blow my budget for the entire trip."

And she had an excuse to spend more time with Adam, do all she could to help him recover.

"Are you sure you truly don't mind doing the work?"

"I don't mind. Gives me something to do. The Army insisted on a medical discharge. I have no idea what to do for the rest of my life since I've lost the only job I've ever wanted." Hurt and loss knifed through his voice.

What could she say to ease his angst? Reassurance he'd find another job would be as fake as telling him he'd ride again. The pain in his words decided for her. She'd stay.

"Thank you for your willingness to help with the bike. I'm happy to assist with the work, of course. Saving on the repairs means staying at the motel won't totally demolish my budget."

Not *totally*. But close.

Adam nodded. The measuring glance he cast her suggested he wasn't sure saying what he planned to was wise. "There's another option for accommodation, I guess. You met Mom when she stayed with me at the hospital."

She closed her eyes and pressed fingers to her temples, searching for the name of the sweet caring woman who'd prayed right out loud at her son's bedside. "Marlene?"

"Yep." He nodded. "I live in an apartment behind the house, and only one of my sisters is still living at home. So there are a couple of spare rooms. Mom won't mind you staying." The words emerged thickly as if dragged from him. Impossible to guess if he hoped she'd agree or hoped she wouldn't.

Torn, Lainie chewed on her knuckle again. If she stayed with his family, they'd be pushed together even more. Maybe she *should* simply ride on and hope for the best.

Then she realized. While they'd worked on the bike, she'd seen the Adam she remembered. Focused, sure of himself, determined. No trace of the despair and deadness that concerned her when he'd arrived at the workshop.

She'd prayed for a way to help him, and it seemed God actually answered her prayer for once. Refusing would be wrong.

Staying could have benefits for them both. Save the charity a chunk of money, and support Adam in finding his sense of purpose and worth again. *Please, God?*

Peace about the decision flooded her. "Okay. As long as your mom really *is* happy having an unexpected guest. And I'd be glad to contribute. I'll help out with groceries, at least."

"I doubt Mom will accept that. But she'll be glad to have you stay. I'll call her now, so you know for sure." He tapped his cellphone.

If Marlene truly *did* welcome her, only one doubt lingered.

After a few weeks with Adam, how would she manage to leave?

CHAPTER FOUR

ADAM WAITED for Mom to pick up his call. She'd expect him to offer the usual Sweetapple Falls hospitality and ask Lainie to stay. If he were honest with himself, he wanted her to stay, too.

But he wasn't much of a cook, so he often ate meals with his family. Getting through weeks with Lainie in the house as well as working with her on her bike would stretch his acting ability to the limit.

If he had any acting ability to stretch.

How could he do it without her realizing how he felt about her?

Not to mention, would she be one more person to drive him nuts insisting he needed looking after?

He loved his family dearly, but if Mom hadn't spent so much time, expense, and effort getting an accessible apartment built and ready for him while he was stuck in rehab, he'd move somewhere else to escape their constant fussing.

Too late to back out now.

When he'd seen how Lainie's shoulders tensed and her face crumpled as she calculated the motel cost, he *had* to offer. Besides, if he hadn't, the expense might have made her choose to keep riding.

He had a basic duty to help a lone woman traveler stay safe and avoid a risky breakdown.

That's all.

Good excuse, Davis. Keep repeating it. You might manage to fool yourself.

Mom, of course, said yes.

Plus, a whole lot more. Enough to reassure Lainie, able to hear

Mom's excited words pouring through the cellphone speaker, she wasn't just being polite. Always hospitable, Mom jumped at the chance to help a nurse who'd cared for him.

"Bring her over now, if you want. I'll lay an extra place at the table for lunch and get a bed made up. She was so kind when I visited with you. All the nurses were, of course, but some stick in my mind more than others. You know how it is."

He knew. Better than he wanted, and *way* better than he wanted Mom or Lainie to guess. Mom would be fast enough to pair them up even without realizing how he felt.

Mom ended the call, and he winked at Lainie. "What did I tell you?"

"Okay, okay. You convinced me. You want the bike to work on. Your mom wants me to stay." Laughing, she raised her hands in surrender. "Free labor on the bike, free accommodation, and such a welcome from your mom. I'd be crazy to refuse. How far is the house?"

"Just on the next block. Walking distance."

He didn't miss the doubtful glance she cast him.

"I made it here okay. I'll make it back, too." He grimaced and pointed to his crutches. "My constant companions. At least they're a step up from the walker I used when I first got out of the wheelchair. If my balance was better, I'd try to get by without any aids. Plenty of amps do."

Bitterness seeped into his voice. Asking the "Why not me?" he'd almost added was a fast track to the self-pity he loathed even worse than sympathy.

Why had God allowed it to happen?

Why keep him here in this pathetic imitation of life when his buddies all died?

Why bring Lainie back into his life, single and unattached, sweet and lovely as ever, when he had nothing to offer her?

As usual, God provided no answers.

Mom and Pastor Dan claimed he needed to trust God had a purpose. If He did, He sure wasn't sharing any information.

Lainie's brow creased as if he'd said all that out loud. "You can't compare your recovery to someone with only an amputation. It's naturally going to take you longer to get there than them. Considering the extent of your injuries, it's needed plenty of grit and courage to get where you are."

Memory shadowed her face. She'd cared for his wounds from when he'd first been medevacced out of Germany right through till she left the hospital. Probably a good thing he remembered nothing of his early treatment or those first weeks in the ICU.

He snorted. "Necessity. Nothing courageous about it."

A militant gleam sparked her dark-blue eyes, and she opened her mouth to argue. Then a loud tooting horn interrupted her.

A pickup stopped outside, and two women jumped out. Sally-Ann and Bluebell. He barely stifled a groan, hoping they were here for Tom's report on the rust bucket Blue called a car and not another do-gooding mission.

The relentlessly positive pair should stick to running the youth group and Sunday school. Stop trying to convince him life was all rainbows and flowers.

Of course, rather than going with her friend to talk to Tom, Sally-Ann made a beeline for them. This time Lainie and her bike trailer magnetized her inquisitive gaze, not him.

"Hello. Are you new to Sweetapple Falls? I'd like to welcome you and invite you to join us in church on Sunday. You can't miss finding it. The blue building with the white steeple. You'll pass it on your way to the central part of town. I'm Sally-Ann Jeffries, the youth pastor. Nicknamed the Salvation Army by those who don't attend church often." The glance she threw him as she thrust out a hand left no doubt who she referred to.

Lainie smiled politely at the girl's torrent of words and shook the proffered hand.

Chattering on without leaving any room for a reply, Sally-Ann peered at the bike and trailer. "'Round-America tour. Wow, so you ride this big motorbike and tow that cute little trailer? What an adventure! Aww, but that means you're just passing through. Shame. I really hoped you'd join us in church on Sunday morning. And tomorrow night at the Pony Express for our karaoke, if you want. You'd enjoy it, for sure."

Finally, her onslaught of cheerfulness paused long enough for Lainie to speak.

"I'm Lainie Sullivan. Thank you for the welcome. I'm having bike problems" — she cast a sad glance at the bike — "so need to stay a while. I'll gladly attend on Sunday. And the Pony Express is…?"

"It's on the next block." Sally-Ann jerked a thumb over one shoulder. "Really *was* the Pony Express office, once upon a time. Now it's a bar. They do karaoke on Thursdays. Everyone goes."

"I don't —"

Her airy wave cut off Lainie's refusal. "You don't need to be able to sing. Most of us can't. And you don't need to drink liquor, either. Most of us don't. The bartender makes fabulous nonalcoholic cocktails. Please say you'll come." She cast a glance at Adam. "You should come, too, Adam."

He shook his head. Sally-Ann didn't give up. Why couldn't people accept he just wanted to be left alone?

Sighing, she raised her eyes heavenward as if uttering an exasperated prayer, but let it go. "Lainie, if you're here long enough to do a talk about your tour to my youth group, that would be great. Pastor Dan will probably invite you to speak to the church, too."

Lainie nodded and reached into her pocket. "Here's my business card with my contact details. Adam thinks the repairs might take a couple of weeks. I'll be glad to speak, if we can set it up for before I move on."

The thought of returning to his colorless existence once she left hollowed his chest and belly. The only times he'd felt truly alive since his injuries were when Lainie was around. Like she was some happy pill, a painkiller for his heart and mind.

Not what he wanted.

He'd weaned himself off the stronger pain meds fast. After seeing guys leave the hospital hooked on the stuff, he didn't want to risk it. Being dependent on anyone or anything wasn't for him.

Including letting himself depend on Lainie.

He tuned back into Sally-Ann's chatter. "So, I'll talk to Pastor Dan about the church schedule and let you know. Where are you staying? Do you need a couch to sleep on?"

Lainie threw him a questioning glance.

There was his chance — less time with her. Instead, a firm reply jumped from his lips. "Mom's excited to have Lainie stay. Already making up a spare room."

Not the way to stop himself from wanting her.

Sally-Ann grinned. "Marlene will take good care of you. Eight p.m. tomorrow at the Express, Lainie. And you make sure to come to church with your mom on Sunday, too, Adam. Looks like Blue is done talking with Tom. Gotta go. See ya!"

Without waiting for a reply, she hurried back to Tom and her friend, waved, then jumped in her pickup.

Lainie stared after her, open-mouthed. Sally-Ann had that effect on people. "Oh my. Is she always so enthusiastic?"

"Yep. And so is Bluebell. Little rays of sunshine combined with every twinkling light on the town Christmas light route. All the time." He rolled his eyes. Impossible to dislike either of the girls. They meant well, but they didn't know when to stop.

"Bluebell." Lainie boggled. "Seriously?"

"Seriously." He almost resisted rolling his eyes this time. "Except Blue is never serious. You'll find out when you get to know her."

She laughed. "Well, a girls' night out might be good for me. It's been a long time since I just hung out with friends. I haven't been to church for a while, either. Not since…" Closing her eyes, she trailed off.

He guessed what came next. Not since her dad's funeral.

They'd both lost things. Big, important things. Him — his buddies, his leg, and his Army career. Her — a father and a fiancé. Not that the fiancé was worth her shedding a single tear over.

But hard to keep believing "Jesus Loves Me, This I Know" when real life smacked you in the face so hard.

Maybe Blue and Sally-Ann could. Mom seemed to.

He couldn't. Not anymore.

Opening her eyes, Lainie pasted on a smile. "How about you?"

"I haven't been on a girls' night out in a long time, either."

Shaking her head, she groaned. "C'mon. You know that's not what I meant."

"I still go to church now and then." He shrugged. "For Mom's sake. She doesn't miss a Sunday. If I stopped completely, she'd worry."

The last thing he wanted was anyone else telling him he ought to go to church more often. Before Lainie could say anything, he got in first. "Mom will be getting ready to serve lunch. I'll grab my crutches, and we should go." He clicked the office chair brakes, so the chair didn't roll away when he got up, leaving him flat on his butt.

She reached out to stop him when he moved to stand. Her gentle touch on his bare arm felt way better than it should. The air caught in his lungs, and he tensed but didn't pull away.

"Is there room at the house to park my trailer?"

He breathed again only when she moved her hand to gesture toward her trailer.

For a moment, he almost wished he did still have faith, so he could ask God to help him get through these weeks with Lainie. Once, he would have believed she'd been brought back into his life for a reason. "Sure. There's space in the garage."

"Can I use my bike to move it? I'm not sure I can haul the trailer so far on my own." Her fingers hovered over the lever to lower the hoist.

Working together, they got the bike back on its center stand.

Once the bike stand whirred into place, Lainie swung her leg over the saddle with practiced ease, started the engine, and moved the bike back. Reverse gearing. The modifications her father added must have cost a packet.

He scooted the chair toward his crutches. Time to get real and stop wishing he could still ride.

By the time he walked back, Lainie had the trailer hitched and stood beside the bike. "Would you like to share a ride home? If you can lift your new leg high enough?" Anxiety creased her brow as she peeped at him.

Getting on her bike wasn't wise. Neither was wrapping his arms around her waist to stay on it. Fast tracks to frustration. Two passions, both out of his reach.

But forget wisdom. She'd be here no more than two or three weeks. Why not grab the chance to be on a motorbike again while he could? So he'd miss riding his Buell more because of it? He'd dealt with worse things. And he'd deal with Lainie leaving when it happened.

Awkwardly, hoping he didn't accidentally nudge the release button on his leg and send it flying off, he swung it over the saddle and moved the artificial foot till his boot heel caught on the foot peg. Being on a bike again, even in the wrong seat, felt great. Provided he didn't think about all he'd lost.

When Lainie clambered onto the bike to sit in front of him and he slipped his arms around her slender waist, the real battle began.

The battle to ignore the sweet raw sensations rioting through him. He'd learned to switch off pain and hunger. This should be no different.

But it was.

Switching off what he felt for Lainie was harder. A whole lot harder.

CHAPTER FIVE

AS SOON AS ADAM reached his arms around her, Lainie realized her mistake.

Without the leather jacket she normally wore when riding, only thin layers of fabric separated their bodies. Too late now to make an excuse and go back to grab her jacket. With unexpected heat setting her skin on fire, she wouldn't be cold. Her T-shirt and light sweater weren't nearly enough to armor her against her reaction to him.

She felt his warmth. She felt the rise and fall of his chest against her back as he breathed. She felt her awareness of him as a singing joy pulsing through her veins.

And she'd seriously underestimated how intense being so close to him would feel.

Something she'd never felt for any other man.

If this was how a woman was supposed to feel for the man she married, maybe Michael had done her a favor ending things. Despite the stinging dismissal still echoing in her brain — *any nurse will do.*

But she shouldn't be feeling this for Adam. Not now and probably not ever.

Not when she'd promised Dad she'd fulfill his dream.

Not when Adam was a patient. Okay, technically an ex-patient. The sense her feelings were unprofessional lingered.

And most of all, not when Michael made her doubt that any man would love her for herself. Patients *did* imagine they'd fallen for their nurses. She mustn't believe for one moment that the warmth she glimpsed in Adam's eyes was anything more.

She hoped for a love like Mom and Dad had. A lifelong tenderness, a sweet affection that never wavered. They'd had something special, worth treasuring. When her engagement ended, Dad reminded her she deserved the same. A man who loved and valued her — cherished who she was and didn't simply want someone to look after him. But would she ever find that man? All her life she'd been valued most for caregiving.

Adam didn't seem Michael's type. Just the opposite.

But she hadn't guessed Michael was that type, either. Her judgment when it came to men clearly couldn't be trusted.

Starting the engine, then slowly turning the bike and trailer around in the big workshop, constantly aware of Adam's presence behind her, she thanked God it wasn't far to the house. Not even a full block. It felt more and more as if she should have accepted Sally-Ann's offer of a couch to crash on. Though he'd mentioned living in a separate apartment, staying with his mom surely meant more time with Adam, too.

But she could manage it. She *had* to manage. Only a couple of weeks. Just avoid any further physical contact and stay focused on her goal.

Moving on and completing the ride. Funding better cancer care and support for patients and their loved ones.

She owed it to Mom and Dad. And to other cancer patients.

Even as she formed the thoughts, she knew there could be more to it.

She swung the bike into the driveway of the Victorian house Adam indicated. Like most of the homes they'd passed, festoons of Christmas lights adorned the wraparound porch. This town took its Christmas lights seriously.

Once she stopped the bike outside the detached garage, as close as she could get to the house's side entrance, Adam pulled his arms away from her waist. Swinging her leg across the saddle, she dismounted, and the breath she'd been holding escaped her.

Relief? Or disappointment?

She knew which one it *ought* to be.

Adam maneuvered himself down from his perch. Good, he'd managed without her needing to offer the help she knew he'd refuse.

Marlene hurried from the house with a bounce in her steps far younger women might envy, though she must be nearing sixty. Only the gray streaking her soft brown hair betrayed her age. A welcoming grin wreathing her face, she ran to Lainie and wrapped her in a warm hug.

Lainie returned her hug, then stepped back.

The older woman kept her hands resting on Lainie's shoulders. "Welcome to Sweetapple Falls and our home. I'm sorry your bike needs these repairs. But it's a blessing to have the chance to see you again and be of some help. You and the other nurses... without the care you all gave Adam..." Closing her eyes, she covered her mouth with one hand and ducked her head.

"Mom..." Concern roughened Adam's voice, but he didn't step away from the bike, keeping one hand pressed to the saddle.

Lainie edged nearer to Marlene and touched the older woman's arm, as she'd done so often in the hospital. Remembering those weeks when Adam hovered between life and death would be a nightmare for any mom. "It's so kind of you to permit me to stay. I'm sorry if me being here brings back upsetting memories."

Marlene raised her bowed head. The smile wobbled back to her lips, though her over-bright eyes glowed less warmly than before. "I have my son. Nothing else matters."

"Would you rather I stayed somewhere else?" She had to ask. Maybe that would have been the wisest choice all along.

"Of course not." Marlene shook her head vigorously, dislodging strands of hair from her loose updo. "I would have scolded if Adam hadn't offered you a room in this home. We have plenty of room, and you're always welcome. Come in. We can talk over lunch. Your things can wait till later."

Lainie turned to Adam, standing beside the bike with one hand resting on the seat. He still hadn't moved.

Guilt twisted her. How could she not have guessed his problem sooner?

"I'm sorry, Adam. I should have realized. We left your crutches back in the workshop. Do you have a spare set in the house?"

Marlene rushed back to her son. "I should have noticed, too. I was so happy to see Lainie. And so glad to see you on a motorbike again. When I heard the engine, I got that 'Here's Adam!' feeling I always had when you rode in. I know how much you miss —" Her words stopped as if she realized reminding him he couldn't ride his beloved bike might not be the best idea.

Lainie wondered the same before offering him the choice to ride the short distance together. Not just being on a bike again, but not being the one in control might be difficult for him. Some men hated being a passenger.

Especially when they were used to riding themselves.

The furrows around Adam's eyes deepened in a hint of a grimace, but he said nothing.

And now she wondered something else. She'd thought accepting his help with the bike repairs would help him. But would that, too, torment him with memories of what he'd lost?

"We should get a second set so you have spares. Adam, take my arm. Better still, lean on your lovely nurse." Marlene's satisfied nod suggested she thought it a wonderful idea. Lainie hadn't missed the older woman's quick glance at her left hand to check for a ring.

Cringing inside, Lainie kept her polite expression firmly in place. They hadn't been nurse and patient for almost a year. The last thing she wanted was Adam seeing her as his nurse.

Or to see herself as his nurse.

Though maybe sticking to that would be safer. Help keep her wayward emotions under better control. She couldn't risk falling in love with another disabled guy who might simply want a caregiver, any more than she wanted to risk the bike breaking down miles from anywhere.

She didn't want to risk falling in love, period.

Twenty-five states to go in her tour. Besides, she couldn't be sure if anyone loved her for herself or just loved her for her ability to care for them. She'd been a caregiver since age ten. Maybe that was all she'd ever be loved for.

As if Adam *was* still her patient, she offered her elbow, bending it as far away from her body as she could.

His overall strength and his control of his prosthetic leg hadn't appeared so poor he'd need her arm around him as some patients did. Probably, he didn't need anything to lean on for support. He simply needed a hand on something stable to override the mixed-up messages his blast-damaged balance system sent out.

Though thinking of herself as "stable" right now didn't make much sense. Her feelings for Adam had her anything but.

With a smile as falsely polite as her own, he held her arm. They paced toward the house, and she struggled to suppress the warm sensations his touch raised.

Focus on assessing his progress, just as she would with any other patient.

Seemed her hunch was correct. No support needed, only something or someone to act as a guide. His touch stayed light. He wobbled once, windmilling his free arm, but corrected himself.

When they reached the porch, he shifted his hand to the wall. "I can manage now. Thanks."

"You're welcome." Surely, those words never sounded so fake with her other patients.

Marlene waited in the doorway, a relieved smile replacing the concern furrowing her face as she'd watched her son walk. "Is Tom following you?"

Adam shook his head. "He has a rush job, so he's working through lunch."

"Not healthy." She tsked. "I'll make him some sandwiches." Then Marlene sighed as angry childish voices rose inside the house. One of those did-so-did-not squabbles that might go on indefinitely.

"Sorry, Lainie. It may be a little loud in here." She rolled her eyes at the understatement. "I should have warned you, I'm minding the grandkids this afternoon. That's Marty and Treeva you can hear. Petra asked me to apologize that she couldn't stay to greet you. The school sent the kids home at noon for staff training, and because she's a teacher there, she had to rush back."

Lainie couldn't quite recall Petra. She'd met Adam's sisters, but only briefly. "I'm sure I'll see her again while I'm here. The bike will take weeks to fix. I feel I'm imposing on your kindness to stay so long."

"Not at all." Marlene beamed. "I'm happy to hear it will be a longer stay. You're welcome here for as long as you need."

The children's escalating shouts almost drowned out her last words.

Pressing fingers to her brow as she shook her head, the older woman pursed her lips. "Why today, of all days, Lord? Son, please show Lainie to the table. I'll go find out what that's all about, then get them ready for lunch." She hurried indoors.

Adam followed more slowly, keeping a hand on the wall, and once in the kitchen, the counter. Lainie trailed a step behind, watching for signs he might need assistance. With something to orient him, he seemed okay.

Glancing around the cheerful yellow and blue open-plan room, kitchen on one end, dining table the other, she smiled. So obviously a family home. Children's artwork covered the huge refrigerator, and toys overflowed a bushel basket in one corner. Marlene would be a wonderful grandmother.

The gray-muzzled black Labrador lying on a rug in the center of the room whined hopefully as he stared up at Adam.

"Sorry, Nosy. No petting unless you stand up. You know I can't bend over now."

"Nosy?" She bent to pet the friendly dog, giving him a scratch behind the ear. He thumped his tail in thanks.

Adam shrugged, lips quirking. "When he was younger, he loved sticking his nose into everything. Unless it's food, he's too old and lazy to be curious now."

"You're a good boy, aren't you, Nosy?" The dog thumped his tail again as she gave him an extra scratch.

"Mom's big orange tabby Oscar is usually in here, too. He'll be around somewhere. Probably hiding from the kids."

Lainie chuckled. "Good thing I like kids *and* pets."

"We'd better sit before the terrible two arrive." He nodded to the dining table. Despite the name he gave them, his eyes twinkled with obvious affection for his sister's family. He teetered as he abandoned the counter's support to take a few steps to the table, but righted himself before her outstretched hand reached him.

He must have noticed her movement. One hand resting on the big table, he turned to her. "I'm fine."

"You can manage." Smiling, she finished his catchphrase for him.

"Glad we got that straight." His dry tones made it hard to be sure if he was joking or serious. Trailing his hand along the chair backs as he moved, he selected one and sat. "You can see Marty's and Treeva's places. Anywhere else is fine to sit."

Lainie pretended to pout. "Awwww. I thought the *Frozen* place setting was for me."

Joke. Not because she *wanted* to sit beside Adam.

He chuckled. "You can try. But I'm guessing Treeva won't be happy."

Right on cue, a blonde girl, her lower lip protruding sulkily, ran into the kitchen. "Won't be happy about what, Uncle Adam? Marty cheating? He did, and it wasn't fair." Then discarding her grievance, she stared up at Lainie. "Hello. I'm Treeva. I'm seven and a half. Mommy told me she named me for Grandpa Trevor because he was a very special person and I am, too. But Trevor is a boy's name, so she made me Treeva. And she named my brother for Grandma Marlene."

"Treeva is a very pretty name." Lainie smiled at the chatty child. "That's like the reason for my name. I'm Lainie because my mom was Elaine and Dad wanted a name like hers but different."

The child nodded. "I like your name, too."

Lainie waved at the table. "I was just admiring your lunch things."

Treeva eyed her, blue gaze wide and assessing in her elfin face. Then she nodded. "Because you're a guest, I'll let you have Elsa today. I'll have Barbie instead." She ran to a kitchen cabinet, opened the door, and assembled a collection of bright pink tableware.

Laughing, Adam picked up the child-sized fork, its plastic handle adorned with Princess Elsa's image, and waved it at Lainie. "Be careful what you wish for. You get to eat with this."

She should have been more careful, for sure. But not for the reason Adam thought.

Now she *had* to sit beside him.

"I'm honored to be permitted to use it." She lowered herself into the seat.

As long as she kept thinking of herself as his nurse, she could do this. Just two or three weeks. That's all. She'd use her professionalism like a shield if she had to.

Marlene ushered in a boy not much younger tan his sister, whose red-rimmed eyes suggested he'd been crying. "Marty, you're going to apologize to Treeva now, aren't you?"

Treeva stood glaring at him, arms folded.

He pouted, then complied. "I'm sorry I cheated and then said I didn't."

"And, Treeva, I want you to apologize for calling your brother unkind names. Just because he did something wrong doesn't mean it's okay for you to, as well." Marlene's firm tone made it clear refusal was not an option.

The girl eyed Marty mutinously. "Okay. I'm sorry I called you names. I shouldn't have done that."

Lainie had to cough to cover her chuckle. Treeva's disgusted voice and expression spoke loud and clear.

"Good. Now we can eat. Everyone to the table." Once she and the children were seated, Marlene nodded to Treeva. "What do we do now?"

"We tell God thank you." She frowned for a moment, then nodded. "Can I do it today?"

"Sure, honey."

They all bowed their heads, Adam included.

"Dear God, thank You for giving us enough to eat and thank You for giving me a mom and a grandma who love me and thank You for Uncle Adam and Miss Lainie — and okay, thank you for giving me a little brother, and I'm sorry I called him names. Amen." The sentence emerged at breakneck pace as if it were one long word.

Before opening her eyes, Lainie gave silent thanks of her own. Such wonderful extended family surrounded Adam.

Since Dad died, she had no family. No one and nowhere she truly belonged. A pang of loss bit her.

This could be the place, and these could be the people, a still, soft voice deep inside her whispered.

No, it couldn't be.

Don't tell me that, Lord. I'm willing to learn to trust You again. I'm even willing to believe You brought me here for a reason, to help Adam. But it doesn't mean I'm willing to stay.

Once her bike was back on the road, she had to leave. Get away from Adam and the untrustworthy emotions he stirred in her.

And finish what she set out to do. She wasn't a quitter, and this trip was no exception.

CHAPTER SIX

BY THAT EVENING, Adam couldn't deny Lainie fit into his family like she belonged there. Mom already adored her. Both being nurses probably helped. Though Mom was an LPN, not an RN like Lainie, they still had plenty of shared experiences.

She'd been great with Mom. Great with Marty and Treeva at lunch. Great to work with, when she'd taken the bike back to the workshop so they could start getting the engine out and stripped down ready to send to Sacramento. She seemed to know instinctively what tool he'd want next.

Then tonight at dinner, over Mom's meatloaf and mashed potatoes, Lainie, Mom, and his youngest sister, Hope, chatted as if they'd been friends for years.

Thanks to the lost hearing the doctors said he wouldn't regain, he found following conversations with more than one person difficult. So he hadn't tried. Simply let the women's words flow around him.

He could listen to the sweet rise and fall of Lainie's voice 24/7 and not tire of it.

Still, it could be unwise to spend more time with her than he had to. She'd been burned by one jerk of a guy, who happened to be disabled. Last thing she'd want was to get involved with another. He didn't think he was a jerk, but he sure *was* disabled. Once her bike was fixed, she'd ride on out of his life, and he'd probably never see her again.

But no matter how much he told himself to keep his distance, it didn't work.

Knowing she'd leave soon only gave more reason not to lose a minute with her.

Today, he'd begun to feel alive again.

It wasn't exactly comfortable. More like the sensation of the shot wearing off after dental work.

He should go back to his apartment, like he normally did straight after dinner. Instead, he'd lingered. Done what he could to help clear up. Moved to the living room when they did. Sat half listening while they continued their conversation, Hope stitched her latest quilt project, and Mom knitted a lacy Barbie-pink Treeva-sized sweater.

The knowing glance Mom threw him suggested louder than words she'd guessed why.

Lainie.

Listening more than she spoke, she stroked big orange Oscar, who'd leapt into her lap and curled there as soon as she sat. Clever cat. Something so restful about her. In the hospital, though she knew how to listen, she'd always been doing. Busy the whole time.

Now, he saw a different side to her. One he liked even more.

The warm glow of the Christmas tree lights gleamed on her hair, highlighting the gold in the wavy strands escaping from her messy braid. Those honey strands probably felt as soft as they looked.

Not something he should be thinking of. Lainie was well out of bounds for him now.

As if sensing his gaze on her, she pinned on an almost convincing smile, then quickly turned back to Mom.

He really *should* go back to his apartment.

Tomorrow, they'd be together all day in the workshop again. He'd better summon up all his willpower and make an excuse to avoid too much more time with her. Stay in his apartment and fix his own dinner, rather than eating in the main house like he usually did. He should have started tonight.

So why did he ignore the undeniable knowledge he could start right now if he wanted?

Because he didn't want.

He'd deal with the hurt when she left. Time with her now would be worth a little pain.

Hearing Lainie mention the workshop, he tuned in to the conversation with an effort. "I meant to ask you something. I met the youth pastor there today," Lainie told Mom. "She asked me to join her and her friends for a girls' night out tomorrow. The karaoke. Would you mind if I went?"

So, she was going. He'd wondered.

Mom beamed approval. "Sally-Ann and her friends are lovely girls. They know how to have fun and still behave themselves. You'll be fine with them. Of course, I don't mind you going."

"I usually go along, too. Even though I can't sing a note." Hope giggled. "Neither can most of us there. I'd come with you, but I can't." She lifted the pastel fabric she worked on. "An urgent commission for a baby quilt. The little one arrived sooner than expected. Maybe next week we can all go together. Adam, too, if he wants."

Lainie threw him a questioning glance he had no problem interpreting. *What about you?*

"Adam *never* does now. He has to be dragged out of the house to get him to go anywhere." Concern for him cracked the edges of Mom's laugh. "I wish you'd go along with Lainie, son. Do you good to get out more."

Adam's jaw tightened. He hated people telling him what was good for him. Even Mom. Nothing wrong with preferring to stay home and lift weights or watch TV over watching people drink more than was good for them and then murder perfectly innocent songs.

One of the few times his hearing loss was a blessing.

Then there were the pitying looks and comments. Bad enough at church when everyone was sober. Add a few beers or cocktails and the stuff some folk thought okay to say to him would surely zoom way off anyone's tolerance scale.

Not that everyone there drank. But enough did to make an evening in the bar more like his idea of social hell. Those who didn't drink much were happy-clappys like Sally-Ann and Bluebell, determined to cheer him up.

But tomorrow night would be different. Lainie would be there. Tomorrow night might be the night he surprised Mom. And himself as well.

Not even a single full day with Lainie, and she'd already nudged him out of his apathy.

Something nothing else had done. Not since the Army medical assessors told him he wasn't fit for any military job and they judged he wouldn't ever be. A one-legged combat medic was never going to happen — he knew that. But surely, despite the ongoing effects of his injuries, they could have used him somewhere? Instead, they'd discharged him, dumping him into a purposeless civilian life.

As Lainie said about walking without crutches or a cane, some amps did it. And some amps were allowed back to active duty, too. Just not amps with all his other disabilities.

Problem was, he'd joined the Army right out of school. Never done anything else, apart from help out in the automotive shop for pocket money. Uncle Frank filled him with stories of the family military tradition. Fired him up with the desire to serve his country.

When he'd decided to enlist, Mom worried about him. Though she never tried to talk him out of it, he knew she hoped he'd change his mind. And despite his dedication to his job, he'd ended his Army career in more of a mess than Mom's worst fears.

Once Lainie left, he needed to figure out what to do with the rest of his life. Stop feeling sorry for himself, stop being angry with the Army. Man up and accept his new reality.

Maybe even stop being angry with God.

Lainie shouldn't enjoy working on the bike with Adam so much. Shouldn't enjoy being with his family so much, either. But she did. No amount of kidding herself otherwise would change that.

When the bike was fixed and she moved on, she'd miss this place and these people.

Especially *one* person.

But no matter how she'd miss him, she had to squash those feelings and keep moving on. Still, surely she could let herself enjoy the few weeks they'd have.

Adam's hair flopped forward, and his brow creased in effort as he strained on the wrench with both hands. Tension bulged his biceps and the flexor muscles in his forearms. She held her breath right along with him.

Finally, the stubborn nut shifted. "Got it!" He punched the air in triumph, and she returned his smile with one just as wide and real.

Already, he seemed a different man from the broken and defeated one she'd seen yesterday when she arrived. Energy and interest lit his eyes. An aura of satisfaction at having a purpose again, even though only a temporary one.

Can it stay that way when I leave?

A prayer or a question?

"Adam 1, Gary 0." Her childhood nickname for Dad's bike slipped out.

Laying aside the wrench, he undid the last few turns of the nut by hand before passing it to her. "Gary?"

She placed the nut carefully with the others. The last thing they needed was missing parts when it came time to put the bike back together again. Waiting for replacements would delay her here even longer.

Would that be a bad thing?

Ignore the treacherous thought. Focus on answering his question.

"Gary Goldwing." She patted the handlebars. "I started calling it that as a kid when I helped Dad with the repairs. He said bikes always had girls' names, and it should be Glenda Goldwing. I insisted nope, this one was a boy and his name was Gary. Always made him laugh."

Adam chuckled. "Makes me laugh, too." He hauled himself to his feet, and his face stilled and became serious as his gaze fixed on hers, holding it in a warm intensity she couldn't evade.

Wasn't sure she wanted to, no matter how much she told herself she should.

"Lainie, I can't tell you how grateful I am you came to Sweetapple Falls. Do you know how long it's been since I laughed?" He shook his head, spreading his grease-blackened hands wide, holding eye contact. Somehow, it bound them together in a moment outside of time.

Her heart twisted for him, for all he'd endured. "I can guess." The words emerged as a husky whisper.

"Too long." A smile like the sun emerging from clouds lifted the darkness shadowing his expression. "But in the single day since you arrived, I haven't stopped. And I'm glad to be able to actually feel like laughing again." His head dipped lower, closer, his eyes darkening.

"I...I'm glad, too." She was.

But only one thought filled her mind and stopped her breathing. Was he about to kiss her? And if he was, should she let him?

So many good reasons not to. And just one good reason to surrender to his kiss.

She loved him.

Terrifying, crazy, and wrong as it felt to admit it, she did. The sooner she got out of Sweetapple Fells, the better. But if Adam's lips touched hers, she'd melt.

"Lainie, visitor here for you." Tom's shout from the other side of the SUV he worked on echoed through the workshop.

Adam blinked and staggered a step back, breaking their endless moment of connection.

Good thing. Because God help her, if he'd kissed her, she would've kissed him back. Something about Adam made her long to forget completing the tour. Forget professional ethics. Forget everything but here and now and making him laugh again.

One day here, and she had no idea what was right or wrong anymore.

Swiveling on one foot, she turned away. "Coming, Tom."

Rounding the vehicle, she approached the visitor. A painfully thin boy of twelve or thirteen in a motorized wheelchair decked with almost as many Christmas lights as the storefront. She blinked at the impressive array.

"Josh wants to speak to you." Smiling, Tom jerked a finger toward the boy. "I thought I should check with you rather than just let him come over to your workstation."

"I'm Josh Tanner." Holding out one hard for her to shake, he pushed his wheelchair control, bringing it closer to her.

"Hi, Josh!" She held up her hand to show him the grease and engine dirt staining it. "Better not shake hands. At least, not till I've washed up."

The boy giggled. "I guess not. Mom won't be impressed if I put dirty fingerprints all over our new van. Tom, Dad said to ask if you would mind looking at the van when he comes to collect me. He wants you to check on something."

"Sure. Whenever he wants." Tom gestured around the workshop. "Place looks busy, but those two vehicles are waiting on parts, and Adam is taking care of Lainie's bike."

"Thanks. So that's the errand part done. Now for the fun part." Josh turned to her.

"I'm glad you see talking to me as fun. You probably know I'm Lainie Sullivan since you came looking for me." She smiled encouragement at the boy. "How can I help you?"

"I don't want to get in the way of what you're doing, but I'd like to see your bike and ask you a few questions. Is that okay?" Hopefulness curled the edges of his grin.

"Of course. Though we'll need to ask Adam if he's okay with it, too. I don't want to distract him from what he's doing." She tilted a head to the corner. "Come on over to our workstation."

Josh's wheelchair whirred behind her.

Adam looked up and smiled as they approached. "Hi, Josh. How are things?"

Obviously, they knew each other. Inevitable in a town this size.

"Pretty good, thanks." He made a face. "Better once school breaks for Christmas. Can I look at the bike and ask Lainie some questions while you work?"

"No problem. But where's your video camera? Not like you to leave it behind." A new teasing note edged into Adam's voice. He really *was* healing.

Laughing, the boy pulled a cellphone from his jacket pocket and waved it in one thin, long-fingered hand. "This works nearly as well as the bigger one. Don't leave home without it." He mimicked the well-known credit card ad. "But I haven't asked Lainie if I can interview her yet. You too, Adam. Now you're getting better, can we do another one?"

So Josh had noticed the change in Adam, too. It wasn't just her wishful thinking. Good.

Adam heaved a huge mock sigh. "Another one? I can't imagine your viewers will want to see more of me after last time, but I'll think about it."

"I'll talk you around."

The boy unzipped his thick padded jacket, allowing her to read some the slogan on his T-shirt. It mentioned muscular dystrophy. She'd wondered. Sad.

"What's this about an interview?" she asked.

"I have a YouTube channel, Sweetapple TV." He rolled his eyes and grimaced. "Not the national network talk show I want, but I'm working on it. I film my performances, I film community events, and I interview anyone interesting."

"I'm flattered you think I'm interesting enough to be worth filming."

Adam laughed. "Sorry to pop your bubble, Lainie, but Josh interviews everyone who'll let him. You heard what he just asked me. He's so desperate for someone to interview, he even wants to film me twice."

Josh pretended to glare at him. "It's not like that, I promise. When I heard there was a woman doing a 'round-America motorcycle tour for charity stopped here, how could I *not* want to interview you?"

"News got out fast. It's not much over twenty-four hours since I got here." Lainie grimaced. She wasn't quite sure she liked the idea of being talked about.

"Small-town life." Adam shrugged. "Someone new in town is big news. You'll be big news again in a few weeks when you leave, too."

Hearing Adam say that, so matter-of-fact, stung more than she expected. Her ridiculous contradictory heart.

When she was alone, away from Adam's confusing presence, she'd have to give herself a stern talking-to. Remind herself of all the reasons she really shouldn't fall in love with him.

And she'd have to hope that, this time, her foolish heart would pay attention.

CHAPTER SEVEN

DESPITE HER THOUGHTS, Lainie flashed a bright smile for Josh. The last thing she'd want to do was discourage the enthusiastic boy. He had more than enough discouraging things to deal with.

"So, will you let me interview you?" He tilted his head to one side and gave her a beseeching, puppy-eyed stare. "It shouldn't take long. Dad set up a room at home as my studio. Mom will be there. She'd like to meet you, for sure."

She suspected she was being played, but no matter. The more publicity the tour and Mom's charity got, the better. Even an interview with a teen on a YouTube channel probably no one watched but his friends and family.

"Excellent." Josh's face lit up. "I can help with fundraising. I'll put the link for donations up on YouTube."

"How many followers do you have there now?" Adam asked, looking up from the wrench he expertly wielded.

Josh pulled a face, crinkling his nose like he'd smelled something bad. She expected he'd say twenty or thirty. "It's slowed down a bit." Then he grinned again. "But no big deal if it's slower. It's still growing. I have nine thousand, nine hundred, and eighty-six. Just fourteen more to hit the big 10K. Hopefully this month."

Oops. She'd been wrong about the family-and-friends-only part. Unless he had a *very* big family and a *lot* of friends.

"Wow. Fab numbers. I'm impressed." Shame the charity's

Facebook page didn't come anywhere near that. She'd struggled to reach a thousand Likes.

"Me, too," Josh said, beaming. "I prayed for it to do well, and it did. I still want my own national chat show someday, but in the meantime, this will do fine. Can I ask you something else, too?"

"Sure." She threw the boy a questioning glance, then stepped nearer Adam to take the nut and bolt he held.

He was as careful not to touch her hands as she was not to touch his. Could he react as intensely to them touching as she did? Her hand trembled a little just being near his, and a rainforest's worth of butterflies danced in her stomach.

Impossible to decide whether the idea Adam felt the same thrilled or terrified her.

Probably both.

Realizing she'd missed a chunk of whatever Josh said and had no idea just *what* she'd missed, she faced him again and tuned back in midsentence.

"And I'm ace at writing grant applications. Dad taught me how when he applied for one to get our van. I could do an application for you." Without waiting for her reply, he looked across to Adam. "I bet I could get you one, as well. Get your bike fixed up so you can ride it again."

A shadow crossed Adam's face. "Focus on getting Lainie whatever you can for her charity." Pain rasped in his voice as he spun the swivel chair away from them, hiding his face.

Clearly, the boy's well-intentioned exuberance prodded hard at one of Adam's sore spots. He seemed convinced he'd never recover enough to ride.

She hurried to speak before Josh could ask Adam the inevitable next question — why not let me get a grant for you, too? "Sure, Josh. I'll gladly go along with you trying to get the charity a grant."

"Great! So that's this term's Civics project taken care of. We have to help a charity or do some community service." The boy brushed his thin hands together as if an A on his paper was a done deal. "I might be able to use this to get a Scouts badge, too. You just need to think of something specific we can apply for."

Blinking, she hesitated. She didn't need any time to know what would be the biggest help, but could Josh really get the charity extra funding? He seemed sure of it. And just as full-on in his enthusiasm as Sally-Ann. Maybe it was something in the water here. Maybe God had His hand on this place in a special way.

Whatever it was, it was so real she could feel it. Faith and hope emanated from them both.

Just, feeling as she did about God, she wasn't sure she liked the uncomfortable reminder of how different things used to be. Back when she had faith and hope, too.

She loosed a long sighing breath. "Right now, a payment toward the repairs on my bike engine is my biggest need. It's going to clean out my funds for the entire trip, even if I couch surf everywhere I can and eat nothing but ramen noodles. Is that the sort of thing you could get me a grant for?"

Josh scrunched up his face. "Maybe. Depends how long you're okay to wait. It's taken six months to get our new minibus with the powered lift for old Silver here." He slapped the arm of his wheelchair. "And we probably only got it because Dad said he'd drive other kids to the Powerchair Football tournaments, too. The special chairs we need for it take up even more room than a normal chair."

Emotions tied in knots, she sighed again. If she stayed here longer than a few weeks, she'd never want to leave. Not the town. Not the Davis family. And especially not Adam.

Forget that idea.

Still, no reason not to accept the boy's offer and ask for something else, less time-specific. It wasn't like she'd have anything better to do during the weeks of waiting for her engine.

"Well, it was worth hoping for. Maybe a dedicated website to give information about the charity and to make donations, not just a Facebook page?"

"I can't have a Facebook page yet. Not till I'm sixteen." He crinkled his nose again, then pointed heavenward and laughed. "You won't need to wait six months for funding to get a website. This *has* to be a God thing. Guess what my Computer Studies term assignment is?"

Though she said nothing, her doubts a kid could do what was needed must have shown on her face. And her doubts that God worked like that.

"It's okay. I can make a website." He rushed to reassure her. "I have one for my TV channel with links to my YouTube page. Dad helped me set it up, but I do all the internet stuff by myself now. Get

Adam to show it to you. He has the link."

Adam glanced up from the bike and gave a lopsided smile. "He does have a good website."

"See, Lainie? I told you I could do a website." Triumph flashed in Josh's smile. "If you visit it, you can watch the interview I did with Adam."

"No, you don't want to see that." Adam shook his head. "Visit his site, sure. But *don't* watch my interview."

So, that explained the twisted lips. And she could guess what he didn't want her to see. A reminder of how she'd first seen him yesterday. Defeated, flat, and dull-eyed. A different man from the man she saw today.

You've made a big difference to him. Stay.

A whisper better ignored. She really had to leave before her heart became inextricably tangled with Sweetapple Falls. And with Adam.

Adam could smack himself on the head for his mistake. He really shouldn't have said more about the interview. Lainie's expression suggested that, first chance she got, she'd be looking for it.

She wouldn't like what she saw.

"My bad," Josh said. "I should have waited till you'd been home longer. I could tell you didn't want to do the interview."

Josh was way more perceptive than most kids his age. Most people *any* age. Despite being just as much a little ray of sunshine as Sally-Ann and Bluebell, he had a tad more sensitivity to go with it.

"No, I did not." Adam wasn't sure he wanted to do one now, either.

At least discussing websites and interviews stopped Josh from pushing the point on chasing a grant for his motorcycle repairs. It wouldn't work, even if Josh could secure the funding. If he couldn't ride his Buell on two wheels the way he used to, he didn't want to ride at all.

Too big a reminder of all he'd lost in the blast.

"But there's an easy answer," Josh brightly continued. "Do another interview. Seeing how different you are now, just a month later, might really help encourage people. You can come along when I do Lainie's."

"Okay."

The word popped out of his mouth before he could stop it.

If the kid also guessed how he felt about Lainie and knew he'd just offered the biggest inducement possible, either Josh was scarily perceptive, or his feelings for her were far more obvious than he intended. It had better be the first option.

"Great." Josh beamed. "I'll check with Dad to make sure of when he can help me set up for the interviews. We could even do a joint interview. Lainie was your nurse, right? That would be great. Maybe over the weekend or Monday?"

Lainie glanced at him uncertainly, doubt shadowing her eyes. So she didn't want a joint interview, any more than he did. Reminding her he'd been her patient didn't feel like a good idea. Not when he wanted to ask her to stay.

He raised a hand. "Stop when you're ahead, kid. I'll do an interview, but no joint interview, okay?"

The relieved smile she threw him said he'd read the situation right. She fumbled in her jeans pocket, then frowned at the piece of white card she extracted before handing it to Josh. "Here's my business card. You can call me to let me know the time you want us to be there. Sorry, it's a bit creased."

He shrugged as he accepted it. "I can still read the number, so it's fine." Unzipping his padded jacket, he tucked the card in an inside pocket and patted it. "There, now I won't lose it. Though if I do, I'm pretty sure Mom has Adam's mom's number."

"Cool T-shirt." Lainie pointed to the slogan Josh's movement revealed and read it aloud. "I have muscular dystrophy, but it doesn't have me."

Josh grinned. "It *is* cool, isn't it? Logan, a kid I met at the Power Football championships, has one. Except his says spina bifida. I got Mom to make this one for me. MD definitely doesn't have me. So the doctors say I won't make it past thirty?" He waved a hand as if brushing off a pesky fly. "I'm gonna be like Stephen Hawkins and surprise them all. And if they're right, I guess I'll just get to meet Jesus a little sooner."

His sunny smile and airy tone made it sound no more a big deal than a trip to Orchard Bridge, a twenty-minute drive away.

Shame grabbed Adam's gut and squeezed, closing his ears to whatever Josh said next. He'd survived. Okay, with pieces missing, like his balance, a leg, and working eardrums. Josh had already lost far more.

Though Josh didn't have to blame himself for a transport full of buddies dying, either.

Before the flashback could take hold, he focused on his breathing. On the feel of the wrench in his hands and his butt in the seat. Real, solid, here-and-now things, the way his PTSD counselor taught him. Acknowledge the truth. Even if he hadn't been so severely wounded, he couldn't have saved them. Even if the blast occurred right outside a fully equipped combat hospital, the guys would still be dead.

For the first time, he began to believe that.

He'd beat this thing. Just like Josh intended to beat muscular dystrophy.

Josh stopped talking and tilted his head to one side like a little bird, a focused expression narrowing his eyes. Then he smiled. "There's Dad, come to collect me. I can ask him right away when he can help me with the interviews. Be right back."

Adam couldn't hear whatever it was Josh heard. Not even when the white minibus pulled up outside the open workshop door. Another gift of the blast — permanent hearing loss.

Lainie stared after Josh as the kid trundled across the workshop to wait for his father to get out. Tom ambled over to speak to Luke, too.

"Wow. What a brave kid." Wonder touched her beautiful face.

"He is. Though just as much a force of nature as Hurricane Sally-Ann and Hurricane Bluebell."

She chuckled. "I thought the same. Okay, I do feel a bit steamrollered into saying yes to everything. More than a bit. But he's amazing." Her brow creased. "I'm trying to think where I've seen him before. Was he on the TV last year? One of those talent-show things?"

Adam nodded. "Yep. Him winning the Talent Trek northwest final is Sweetapple Fall's biggest claim to fame, next to having the third oldest church west of the Rockies. He calls himself a sit-down comedian. He won enough public vote with his act to convince the judges to let him go through to the grand final. Before he made it there, he got pneumonia and was in the hospital. It was touch and go for a while if he'd make it."

Her lips twisted. She'd nursed him when his survival been touch and go, too.

Time he changed his attitude. From victim to survivor. Because Lainie being back in his life again made him want to survive. Fiercely. Defiantly. Joyfully.

Time he became the man a woman like Lainie deserved. Then, when he had something to offer her, maybe he could ask her to stay.

CHAPTER EIGHT

A FEW HOURS LATER, Lainie sat at a round timber table in the Pony Express with Sally-Ann, Bluebell, and another girl who'd introduced herself as Natalie. The bar wasn't bad. As Sally-Ann said, they had a good range of nonalcoholic drinks, too. The rustic decor and historic memorabilia adorning the rough-cut timber walls gave a relaxed atmosphere. The girls were friendly and welcoming.

But though only a few years separated them in reality, she felt twenty years older than the giggling, overdressed group. Anyone seeing them would assume they'd been drinking, though she hadn't seen them drink anything stronger than slow sips of the fancy mocktails the bartender suggested. She certainly wouldn't be gulping hers. Fancy mocktails came with a fancy price tag.

Neither the drinks nor the women's clothes fit the woodsy, country-style interior. Tiaras, shiny satin, sequins, and jewels dominated the fashion choice. Thankfully, a few women were dressed as simply as she was. But surrounded by such glamor she felt like a reverse fairy tale. An ugly duck in a gaggle of swans.

Maybe she should have accepted Hope's offer to loan her a sequin-encrusted evening frock so she could play dress-up along with the others, instead of sticking to her basic jeans and sweater.

Maybe, she shouldn't have come.

And *definitely* she should stop watching the door, hoping Adam might surprise them by turning up. Unlikely, given how quiet he'd been over the family dinner before disappearing to his apartment.

That didn't alter how she wanted him to appear. She couldn't deny choosing the most flattering of her three pairs of jeans and her prettiest sweater. Or going to more trouble with her hair and putting on a little makeup. Just a slick of lip gloss and mascara.

No big deal. She would've done that for a girls' night out, anyway, right?

Nice try, but she couldn't fool herself.

Taking another sip of her mock Bellini, peach nectar and fizzy mineral water in a sugar-frosted champagne glass, she dragged her focus back to the girls' discussion. What songs they should sing.

"Or more accurately, wail and shout, not sing." Natalie laughed. "We should do 'It's Raining Men' together, that's our signature tune after all. That can come last. But what about our solos? Lainie, you're newest, want to go first?"

Recoiling, she put down her drink and raised her hands in horror even less mock than her drink. She'd just about managed to calm her nerves when giving her fundraising talks. Getting up on stage and singing was a whole different deal.

"Hey, give me a break, guys. My first week here, maybe I should ease in gently? I'm a nurse, not a singer," she intoned her best Doc McCoy. "How about I just shout encouragement from the sidelines? I'm good at that."

They all laughed. "Nice try, but so not going to happen." Sally-Ann winked. "No one minds if you're not a good singer. And you don't have to be able to sing a note to be as good as us. I wasn't joking when I told you none of us can sing. You'll wish you brought earplugs with you when we do our solos. At least join us in our group songs?"

Lainie smiled, conceding defeat. "Okay. I can probably yell along with you through 'It's Raining Men'. But that's all."

"Okay!" Bluebell victory punched the air. "We won't pester you anymore about singing a solo. When you see how much fun we have, I guarantee you'll *want* to sing. Now we just have to decide who does what solo."

While the girls huddled into a vigorous discussion over their favorite songs, Lainie sipped again on her sweet drink and let their words form background noise. Being with other women made her realize how lonely she'd been since leaving Bethesda to care for Dad.

So much she'd left behind. Her work, her church, her friends, and her fiancé.

And since then, all those long days and nights alone with Dad toward the end. The isolation of life on the road, of fleeing town every night or two. Being here with the girls, in the workshop with Adam, and at home with Marlene and Hope, she hadn't felt that loneliness once.

Already thinking of Sweetapple Falls as home scared her. As an Army brat, she'd never really set down roots. She'd imagined she had in Bethesda, but how easily uprooted she was.

The thought of coming back after she finished her tour nagged at her. Could she risk setting down roots, when she could be uprooted all over again? Could she risk her feelings for Adam, when they still felt uncomfortably unprofessional? And especially when, after Michael, she couldn't be sure her feelings were real?

Maybe Michael had been right. Maybe she *was* codependent. A professional carer, looking to find meaning and purpose as a caregiver in her off-duty hours, too. That thought nagged at her even more than the thought of coming back to Sweetapple Falls.

Safer to keep moving on and not look back. Once her bike was roadworthy again, she'd leave. Her heart proved itself untrustworthy. She'd simply trust her head.

The only safe way to do it.

Adam wobbled into the bar on his crutches. His first visit since coming home. He wasn't about to risk going down the alcohol route he'd seen too many other wounded warriors take. But tonight was different. Lainie would be here.

He hadn't changed into anything fancier when he'd gone back to his apartment after dinner. His plain white shirt, gray sweater, and blue jeans would have to do. Some of the women made the most of the weekly opportunity to glam it up, Hope's words for her and her friends' excesses of sequins and satin.

Thankfully, the dress code at the bar was more casual for the men.

Besides, Lainie had seen him in a hospital gown, smashed-up, unconscious, and probably drooling. Putting on his best clothes and splashing on aftershave wouldn't impress her. He'd simply go as he was, his normal, everyday self.

Unlike Tom and his other cousin Mitch, standing one on each side of a woman nearer Tom's forty than his thirty. Hard to miss, with a silver plastic tiara perched on red hair streaked with electric blue to match her dress. Was it one of Petra's teacher friends? Rusty, Dusty, something like that?

Both men were way more dressed up than usual for a Thursday night, and both appeared to be vying for her attention. Good to see Tom getting over his divorce at last.

Tom waved and pointed to an empty seat beside them, calling him over. Adam replied with a headshake. They didn't need another man at their table. And he wasn't here to see any other woman. Only Lainie.

Besides, the seat Tom indicated had its back to most of the room. Instead of sitting, Adam propped himself against a pillar, took his weight on his good leg, and scanned the bar. He spotted Pastor Dan. He spotted a few of his old buddies, guys he'd barely seen since coming home from rehab. And finally, he spotted Lainie.

Right at the front, seated at a table near the stage with Sally-Ann and Bluebell, cheering on Natalie as the other Sunday school teacher began to sing — if you could call it that. She massacred the song so badly he couldn't tell for sure *what* song. He just knew was what it wasn't. Not "It's Raining Men" a song the girls usually did at least once and sometimes more. "Firework"? Possibly. He really wasn't into this style of music.

While Nat and the other two wore glittery evening dresses, Lainie simply wore jeans and a sweater. And she looked more beautiful than every woman in the room combined.

He loved seeing her face lit up and alive. In the hospital, she'd been caring, compassionate, and always professional. Filled with quiet optimism and faith, ready to chuckle and smile, but the circumstances made showing too much joy inappropriate. When she'd arrived at the workshop yesterday, grief for her dad had been uppermost.

Now, he saw happiness and fun. If ever a woman deserved to be loved, she did. He wasn't the man for her. How could he be? He stared down the barrel of the truth he'd recognized earlier. He'd become an angry, bitter recluse, blaming everyone else for what was wrong with his life. Unless he changed big time, Lainie deserved better.

Far better.

Her fiancé hadn't been it. But someplace, sometime, she'd find the right one.

People kept approaching him to talk. He wanted to pretend the karaoke noise prevented him from hearing them. Normally, he would.

It wasn't too far from the truth. In somewhere like this with a lot of background noise, deciphering words became even more challenging. But since they seemed so pleased to see him, it felt ungracious not to manage a few words for each. He noted the friends who didn't approach him, too. The ones who'd been awkward and embarrassed.

Next time, he'd have to take the initiative and speak to them.

Gene, an old buddy from their high-school football days, came over with a Coke bottle in each hand and offered him one. "I figured you wouldn't be able to carry a drink with your crutches. Good to see you back in the land of the living."

With the wall to stop him unbalancing, he could loosen one hand from the crutch grip and accept the soda. He saluted Gene with it. "Thanks. So that's what you call it? Living?"

His friend laughed. "That probably depends on who's singing."

Finally, Nat ended her song and tumbled back into her seat, helpless with laughter. The girls pushed and dragged Lainie up on stage. "We've all sung. It's your turn!" They stomped their feet and slapped their hands on the table. "Lainie, Lainie, Lainie."

She blinked, then straightened her back and raised her chin as the emcee tapped on the microphone. On the spotlit stage, the lights gleaming on her hair and adding sparkle to her wide eyes, she looked beautiful. Bambi-in-the-headlights beautiful, but still beautiful.

"Looks like Sweetapple Falls and the Express are blessed with another new lady tonight," Doug announced into his mic. "And somehow, I'm guessing her name might be Lainie. Why don't you tell us a little about yourself?"

"Um, yes, I'm Lainie...." She took the mic he passed her and quirked an uncertain smile. Clearly, unprepared for this. "My name is Lainie Sullivan. I'm a registered nurse, and I'm on a tour of every mainland US state, raising money for cancer nursing care, in memory of my mom and dad who both lost their battles with cancer." She looked around the bar. "Okay, I didn't plan for it, but this is where I launch into a speech. Mom was a nurse like me, and after she died, it became Dad's dream to do the ride they'd one day hoped to do together. He set up this charity for her, to make sure every nurse knew more about cancer care and the needs of people with cancer. Unfortunately, before Dad could fulfill that dream, he fell ill. Our hospital and home nursing services provide great care for most people. But I believe every cancer patient deserves access to nursing support at every stage of their cancer journey. I cared for my father, and I just hate thinking of the people who don't have anyone and feel alone and unsupported as they make that journey."

Emotion trembled her voice and shone in her tear-wet eyes. No wonder this tour meant so much to her. No wonder continuing with it meant everything to her.

"I remember one man in particular, who we met in the chemo clinic. He was so grateful to talk to us because he said no one in his life understood what he was experiencing. And worse, none of them would talk with him about the cancer, like if they pretended it wasn't there it would go away. He said how he'd wake up in the middle of the night and he'd want to talk and there was no one he could talk to. How he felt the loneliness ate at him just as much as the cancer did. He lost his battle a few weeks before Dad."

Visibly pulling herself together, straightening her shoulders and swallowing hard, she raised the mic to her mouth again.

"So the Elaine Sullivan Cancer Nursing Fund aims to make sure every person in the country with cancer, or caring for a loved one with cancer, can access nursing telephone support whenever they need to. Listening, giving information, connecting people with the right local services to help. Dad envisioned setting up a whole new network to do this, but it's more cost effective to fund extra nursing hours in the existing telephone nursing services and hospice services. That way, we help more people." As she spoke, her voice grew in confidence and volume.

Another side of Lainie he hadn't seen before. He stared at her. She really was incredible.

She grinned. "I'm sure you guessed it was coming. This is the bit where I hit you up for money. I don't use any of the charity's funds to cover the costs of my trip, so all the money donated goes directly toward funding nursing care. If anyone would like to give to the fund, just drop by the Automotive during their opening hours. I'll be there all day tomorrow. Is that okay?" She glanced to Tom for approval, and he nodded.

"Sure thing. If Lainie's not there, you know I'll be happy to take your money anytime. I can take it right now if you want."

Laughter rippled around the bar.

Lainie rolled her eyes and waggled a finger at Tom. "Don't give your money to just anyone, folks. The charity has 501(c) status so donations may be tax deductible. If you donate, make sure you get an official receipt. I didn't bring any with me tonight, unfortunately. If you want to know more about the charity, my trip, or what we do with the money, just come talk to me. I'll also leave some business cards on the table, telling you how to find the charity Facebook page where you can read more about it and donate online. If you feel moved to give in person, you know where to find me."

"Wow, amazing!" the emcee intoned. "A woman with a mission. And what would you like to sing tonight, Lainie?"

She moved to hand the mic back to him. "No, I'm not going to sing. Thanks for giving me the chance to say a little about Mom's charity."

Both the emcee and the girls had other ideas. He refused to take the mic. The three girls crowded on stage with her and wouldn't let her go.

Lainie rolled her eyes. "Okay. Looks like I have no choice." Her forehead crinkled. "But my mind's gone blank on what song. All I can think of is 'Amazing Grace'."

He shook his head. "I'm sorry, but we don't have that one. Pick something else."

Her smile wobbled, but she lifted a hand. "It's okay. I can sing it without the music if I have to. But this is my first time doing karaoke, so everyone please forgive me if I mess it up."

Closing her eyes, she began to sing, her sweet, clear voice filling the bar with the old familiar words of faith and hope. The girls formed a backing chorus, on tune for once.

"Amazing grace, how sweet the sound, that saved a wretch like me. I once was lost, but now I'm found; was blind, but now I see."

Was that him? He'd surely been wretched. And lost and blind, too?

One by one, the people around him joined in. Voices swelled as if this was the church, not the bar.

In that moment, it *was* a church. Wherever people worshiped God became a church.

Against his will, his heart and his voice sang along, and tears stung his eyes. He hadn't cried once since the blast. Hadn't prayed since the day the docs told him he had to lose his leg. Could be, he should have done both. Could be, God was listening. Could be, unashamed tears made him more of a man, not less.

His scattered thoughts morphed into a prayer.

Okay, Lord. I know we shouldn't ask for signs, but I need You to prove myself to me. If You want me to believe in You again, show me that You do really care, that nothing happens by accident.

As the song ended, Lainie opened her eyes and looked straight at him. Their gazes met and held, and pure joy took her face from beautiful to radiant.

So she was pleased he'd come to the bar tonight.

But was the joy lighting her face merely a caring nurse seeing a patient show signs of recovery? Or could it be the joy of a woman happy to see the man she'd begun falling in love with?

And if it was, where did they go from here?

CHAPTER NINE

"HELLO? Is Anyone here?" The woman's voice echoed from the front of the workshop.

Tom asked them to field any customers who came in while he delivered tractor parts to one of the nearby orchards. Plus, after the karaoke last night, people had called in all morning with donations for her charity. Between that and helping Adam with the bike, they'd been busy.

Adam grimaced as he clicked his chair brakes off and readied to push back from the workbench they'd hoisted her engine onto. To stop him, she rested a hand on his forearm. At the simple touch, a surge of warmth tingled along her skin and heated her face. She jerked her fingers away and ducked her head.

"I'll go speak to her. You've been working hard. It's probably another donation, anyway." Her voice emerged far huskier than she liked. She didn't dare glance at him to check if he'd noticed her betraying blush.

Hadn't she learned yet not to touch Adam unless she had to? She couldn't be the same with him as she was with everyone else.

Her reactions were completely inappropriate. Even *without* touching him.

She didn't want to feel this way. Shouldn't feel this way.

So many reasons she shouldn't.

Today's reminder was Marlene's not-so-subtle hint over breakfast that she'd allowed attraction for a patient in her care to develop into something more — a committed marriage, till death do us part — and she'd be happy to see her son do the same. Good thing Adam breakfasted in his apartment so he wasn't there to hear his mother's words. Or see her blush.

Impossible to retort with what she believed, that professional standards had changed since Marlene married Trevor. Now, when many nurses saw becoming romantically involved with a patient or ex-patient as an abuse of the nurse-patient relationship, a good nurse simply didn't let it happen. So she'd nodded but said nothing.

Shame not one of the nursing websites warning a nurse against it went one step further and said *how* not to. Clearly, how to stop those feelings when they'd already started formed a professional secret she'd somehow missed learning in nursing school.

Her feelings didn't seem to come equipped with an off switch.

"I'm fine," Adam started his habitual reply.

She shook her head. "No, you're not." The dark shadows under his eyes suggested he'd had little sleep. "I'm guessing you had a bad night."

"Not the best." His clipped tone warned her not to question him.

Probably pain kept him awake. Injuries so severe meant a lifetime of pain.

Going to the bar suggested a big step forward in his recovery. But he'd left right after she sang and had been quiet this morning. Perhaps he'd overdone it. All this work on her bike could be too much for him.

Ready to ask about his pain meds, she closed her mouth with a snap. He had the right to choose whether or not to take them. In the hospital, he'd refused the analgesia she'd offered to ease his wound care, resisting her attempts to persuade him. She'd hated inflicting pain on him, though it was necessary pain.

Not just Adam. She hated causing pain for any patient. But the others usually accepted the offered pain meds.

Of course, maybe her singing drove him away. At the time, it felt right. And then her joy to see Adam there overrode everything else. Later, the nasty little doubts started. Could be, she'd made a fool of herself impulsively singing a hymn instead of a raucous pop song like everyone else. People had been kind to join in.

"Hallo–o, I'm looking for Lainie," the voice called again.

She put down the wrench she'd held ready for when Adam next needed it. "One moment. I'll be right with you," she called. Embarrassed to keep the woman waiting so long, she hurried forward.

The thirty-something standing at the entrance beamed and tucked a wayward lock of reddish-brown hair behind one ear. "Hi! Just who I wanted to see."

Lainie smiled a welcome. Could this be another donation? Ten today so far, and the manager at the Pony Express told her to be sure to bring her receipt book with her next Thursday because he'd make it a charity fundraiser. People in Sweetapple Falls were generous, as well as kind.

"Hi!" The recollection of blue streaked hair and a tiara tickled at the edges of her memory. "You were at the karaoke, too, weren't you?" It seemed most of the small town had been.

"I was. I'm Rebecca Matthews. Most people call me Rusty, for obvious reasons." She lifted one auburn tress. As she held out a hand for Lainie to shake, the laughter lines around her hazel eyes crinkled. "I figured anyone gutsy enough to get on stage and sing without the music most of us need to cover our voices was worth getting to know. And deserved a donation, too!" She pulled a checkbook from her big slouchy purse and waved it.

"Thank you. Happy to meet you, Rusty." Lainie warmed instantly to the friendly woman and not just for her donation. "Come into the office. We can use the desk there."

As she walked past, she couldn't resist peeking at Adam. His broad shoulders, his tousled hair, the muscles flexing in his strong right arm as he ratcheted a bolt.

He didn't turn from the workbench. Not even Rusty's cheery, "Hi, Adam!" made him look around.

He just raised one hand in acknowledgment and kept working.

"Looks like you being here is doing Adam good," Rusty said when the door closed behind them. "I work with Petra at the elementary school, and she's told me how worried they all were about him never leaving his apartment. You were his nurse, right?" The inquisitive gleam sparking her eyes suggested she sniffed a potential romance.

Did everyone in town want to play matchmaker? They'd be disappointed.

"Yes, I cared for him in the military hospital. But I won't be here long. Three weeks, tops. Once my bike's fixed, I'll get back on tour. I have a long way to go and a lot more states to visit. Twenty-five, to be exact."

"It's certainly some adventure you're on. But who knows, maybe you'll come back to this part of the world when you're done." Again, those hazel eyes twinkled.

"I doubt it." She tensed, praying Rusty would drop the subject. If she *did* return, what difference would it make? Even if Adam felt the same for her, she couldn't allow it to develop into more. Something in her screamed wrong wrong wrong at her fragile hopes it could.

Pursing her lips, Rusty looked ready to argue. Then she shrugged. "Shame. So, who should I make this out to?" Her pen hovered over her checkbook.

"The Elaine Sullivan Cancer Nursing Fund. Here." Lainie pushed the charity business card across the desk.

Rusty signed with a flourish and slid the check over.

As Lainie filled in her form with the details, then passed the top copy to her, the other woman gazed at her thoughtfully. "Hey, I'm wondering. You want to meet one afternoon next week for a coffee? Maggie's diner down on Main Street is pretty much the only place to go. But the staff are nice, the pie is amazing, and they make good coffee." Rusty glanced at her own glittery fingernails, at Lainie's hands, and laughed. "I was going to say, or visit the nail bar and chat while we treat ourselves to a manicure. But I can see you probably won't go for that."

Chuckling, Lainie examined her short unpolished nails. "Nurses can't wear colored polish on duty, so I've had a manicure exactly once. I didn't get through the day without chipping it. But coffee, for sure. I don't know which day, yet. Depends on how the work on my bike goes."

"No problem." Rusty grinned. "Will you know by Sunday? If you come to church with Marlene, we can talk after and work something out."

"I'll be there," Lainie answered without needing to consider it.

Adam mentioned Marlene would expect it. But she hadn't agreed out of politeness to her hostess. For the first time since her heart broke when God wasn't saying yes to her prayers for Dad, she *wanted* to go to church.

"Great! Gotta go. I have a To Do list a mile long. I'll let you get back to Adam." Smirking, Rusty breezed out of the office.

Lainie sat motionless, hands flat against the cool Formica desktop. Agreeing to attend church reminded her when she last set foot in a house of worship.

Dad's funeral. The pastor claimed God would eventually bring good from everything, even something like this, though we often couldn't see it right away. Caught up in her anger and grief, Lainie saw nothing good in Dad's death. Nothing apart from simply knowing he wouldn't suffer anymore.

But maybe the pastor was right.

She still couldn't see it, but she could accept maybe God *would* show her His purpose was for good. In His own time, of course.

Pushing away from the desk, she stowed the check in her bank bag, then returned to Adam and the bike. He twisted on the chair and gestured at the workbench in an unspoken "Ta-da." Her bike engine, minus the numerous things the rebuild workshop wanted removed.

"You've got it all done already? I'm amazed how fast you did that." She had to put her hands behind her back to resist the urge to hug him.

"Yep. It's done." He waved a grease-blackened hand at the parts. "Ready to pack and send off for the rebuild."

His adorably boyish grin looked so like the ones she remembered. He'd still managed that grin now and then in the hospital, even in the middle of his pain. She hadn't realized how much she'd missed it.

Gratitude blossomed in her heart.

"Thank you." Her words were directed as much to God as to Adam. Moving nearer to getting her bike on the road again was good. Seeing his sweet grin again and the obvious sense of achievement completing the task gave Adam was even better.

"The packaging should be somewhere under the bench. Tom keeps a supply of crates. We need one about so big." He gestured to indicate size. "Labeled J And M Engineering. Maybe nearer the bottom of the stack, if the last motorcycle engine he sent was when I did my bike."

She rummaged through the neatly stacked timber-strengthened boxes for the right one. Together, they packaged the engine.

"I'll wash up, and then get on the computer to finalize the order. Do you have your credit card? You'll need to pay now."

She nodded. "My purse is in the office. And I have a pretty high limit. I don't think my payment will bounce."

His smile widened as he gestured at her bike, now in pieces. "Better not, or we're in trouble." After scooting the chair to the washbasin, he methodically lathered and scrubbed his hands and nails.

Lord, thank You! Adam smiled his old smile. If there's anything I can do to help him heal his worst wounds, the ones that don't show, please tell me. And would You tell me what to do about my feelings for him, as well?

Even if falling for Adam felt wrong, praying again after so long felt right. Another step back to her former closeness with God.

Holding the sink for stability, Adam stood. As he paced to the office with one hand on the wall for balance, she longed to offer him her arm instead, despite knowing she'd get those unwanted tingles again. Her caring instincts demanded she help, not watch him struggle.

Or couldn't he make things easier for her, simply keep scooting around on the old office chair?

But that he wanted to walk without his crutches and without anyone helping him, either, was good and healthy. Tough to stand back, yet respecting his need for independence was the best thing she could do.

Finally seated in front of the computer, he tapped in the company name. "Good, I can arrange for a collection tomorrow." Then he quirked his lips to one side and swiveled the chair to face her. "Sorry I didn't see this on my phone the other day when I scared you half to death with how long it might take. Looks like they offer a rush option. Guaranteed return in three working days from when they get it. I was right in what I told you about the standard job. It's way cheaper, but they say it could take three weeks." He named the different prices.

Her head wanted to spend the extra. Get back on the tour faster. Honor her promise to Dad. Though she'd failed to help him beat the cancer, she wouldn't fail him in this. Plus, she'd leave what she felt for Adam behind.

Her heart insisted on the slower option. Sure, she needed to save money. Sure, her feelings for Adam bothered her. But she sensed some truth to what Rusty said. If staying longer helped lift Adam far enough out of his depression he wouldn't slip back, she'd do it. Wait till she saw more evidence of his recovery.

A good nurse shouldn't feel attracted to her patient.

And a good nurse shouldn't leave her patient till her work was done.

"The regular service will do fine."

Adam's grin as he clicked that option told her she'd made the right decision.

CHAPTER TEN

THOUGH ADAM told himself not to read anything more than a limited budget into Lainie's decision not to take the rapid turnaround on the Goldwing engine, it still felt like a gift worth more than rubies.

One he didn't want to refuse or ignore. Joy and a sense of rightness he hadn't felt for a long time coursed through him. If this time with her really *was* a gift from God, his only response could be to appreciate it.

First step, enjoy whatever time they had together. Until J And M sent the engine back, they'd run out of things to tinker with on her bike. But she'd probably enjoy getting to see more of Sweetapple Falls. Maybe she'd even enjoy her time with him, too.

With that in mind and the bike engine safely dispatched, he tagged along on Saturday afternoon when Hope drove Lainie out to the falls to show her the number-one local beauty spot. His first visit to the falls since he'd been home, though he'd regularly hiked and whitewater rafted along the river in his pre-blast days. In the summer heat or whenever he'd wanted time alone, the cool and shady river gorge had been his go-to place.

He'd resisted going back since he could no longer hike his favorite trail. But giving in to his resistance now would only rob him of time with Lainie. He didn't intend to waste a minute he could spend with her.

Thankfully, the boardwalk from the parking lot gave easy access through the woods to the lookout. Ironic he'd scorned the addition of the railed path when it had first been proposed. Even said that anyone who couldn't hike to the falls had no business being there. Oh boy, he'd had a lot to learn. So much taken-for-granted. Pride and arrogance in the blessing of his effortless fitness. A pride now well and truly humbled.

He calculated exactly when Lainie would first see the view and let the chatting girls lag behind so he'd be there ahead of her. Grinning, he propped against the guardrail and loosened his grip on the crutches to pull his coat tighter against the chill the rushing water created. He breathed deep. Though the platform didn't usually catch any waterfall spray, the air carried the unmistakable tang of wild water.

Good to be back. He'd missed this place. If it wasn't for Lainie, he'd still be wrapped in his self-pity, stuck home in the apartment working out while watching daytime TV.

Here, just as while working on her Goldwing, he felt alive again.

God used Lainie to unlock another stage in his healing. His physical wounds healed months before. But the emotional and spiritual wounds? They'd only just begun to mend.

He twisted as Lainie and Hope drew near to the viewing platform. Any moment now, she'd turn the corner, and the vista cedars had hidden would open in front of her.

Even over the roaring falls, even with his hearing loss, he heard her gasp. Her steps stilled, and she gazed open-mouthed at the majestic cascade tumbling down the cliff face. The town's hidden treasure. A day like today showed it at its best, the sunshine turning each drop of mist into a sparkling rainbow jewel.

He almost laughed at his lyrical comparison. Mrs. Williams, his old high-school English teacher, would be proud of that metaphor. If this kept up, he'd be writing a love sonnet next. Lainie could turn a practical guy like him into a poet.

"So, what do you think?" Hope smiled at her new friend, sure of the answer.

"I'm not sure I've ever seen anything more beautiful." Awe hushed Lainie's sweet voice to a whisper he strained to hear.

I have — you. He didn't voice the thought.

As if she could hug the view, Hope extended her arms. "I stop and stare every time I see it again. I could never leave Sweetapple Falls. I simply love the place too much."

"I love it, too." No point imagining Lainie's words and her

decided nod meant she'd consider staying. Her mission was too important to her.

Though maybe, once she completed her mission, she'd consider coming back.

A guy could hope.

She pulled out her cellphone. "I'll take some pictures to post to Instagram."

"I've posted hundreds." Hope chuckled. "No exaggeration."

After snapping several photos, Lainie tucked her phone in her purse and stood gazing out to the falls. "Amazing. Thank you. Thank you both so much."

"No need to thank me." Hope chuckled. "I come out here every chance I get. You gave me an excuse to get in another visit. Easy to believe in a Creator who loves us when He shows us something like this. "

Lainie's reluctant nod and the uncertainty creasing her brow suggested she was a little less certain. "It's wonderful." She extended a hand over the guardrail, stretching toward the cascade on tiptoe, then pulled her arm back, lips downturned. "Can we get nearer the water? Close enough to feel the spray?"

He threw Lainie's footwear a glance. Hiking boots, exactly like Mom's. Wise move. It wasn't a path for regular shoes, and the water would soak her motorcycle boots.

"Great, you borrowed Mom's boots. Good thinking on her part." His sister beamed approval.

No wonder the boots looked like Mom's. Probably her waterproof jacket was Mom's, as well. Mom took to Lainie like she'd found a fifth daughter.

"Sure, we can get closer. There's a break partway down where you can get closer to the water. This way." Hope pointed off to one side where the trail met the accessible area. "It's not far."

As Lainie followed her to one side of the viewing platform, he weighed up Hope's "not far". When he'd visited last, a couple of hundred yards on a steep muddy path and the rough steps hewn into the cliff had been nothing.

Now, "not far" would be *too* far.

Even last week, bile and fury over having to admit that would've seethed in him. Today, he could accept the fact, even if it didn't thrill him. Time to come to peace with his new normal. Whether he liked it or not, this *was* his new normal now.

"Mind if I sit this one out?" He lifted one crutch and waved it toward the bench overlooking the falls, just a few steps away on the elevated viewing platform.

Hope turned, a hand raised to her mouth, horror at her mistake tightening her face. "Adam, I'm so sorry. I didn't think...."

"It's okay." He smiled, meaning it. The first time any of his family had overlooked his disability. "Honestly, I'd much prefer people forget. I'm still me. Just minus a bit."

"I don't need to get closer." Lainie rushed into apologetic speech. "I've seen the gorgeous waterfall from here. It's enough."

Shaking his head, he gestured again with his crutch. "Sitting with a view like this while you go with Hope will be no hardship."

"Are you sure?" Concern creased Lainie's brow and dimmed her lovely eyes.

"Sure I'm sure. Go for it."

Joy lit Lainie's face, and something warmly appreciative in her gaze showed she'd noticed his attitude shift. But instead of walking away, she spun on her heel and ran to him.

"I'm grateful and glad." Obvious she meant more than for the chance to walk nearer the falls. She tried to grab his hand, but when he couldn't untangle it from the crutch fast enough, she rested one hand on his shoulder and kissed his cheek before stepping back. "Very glad."

A quick peck of gratitude. No more.

But still, the sweet sensation of her lips on his skin spun his equilibrium out of control. Good thing he leaned against the railing.

"Scoot," he growled, emotion hoarsening his voice.

Hope eyed them, speculation gleaming. Mom and his sisters were a little too obvious about their hopes he and Lainie would get together. Their "help" was more likely to make Lainie back off.

He gave Hope his best "shut it, little sis" glance.

Looked like she got the message. Her raised-eyebrow grin promised she'd be on his case later, but she said nothing of whatever she thought about the kiss. Just pointed to the trail. "This way."

As the women disappeared behind the trees, he had to ask.

Lord, I know she's going to leave. I know I have to let her go. But do You need to make it so danged hard?

Despite the need to focus on her footing as Hope led her down slippery moss-covered stone steps, despite the awe-inducing beauty of the falls, despite the squirrels chittering their rebuke, much of Lainie's attention fixed on berating herself. Why had she kissed Adam?

One of those spontaneous, spur-of-the-moment things that were just plain stupid. And once done, impossible to undo.

Though the kiss only lasted a second, probably less, she could still taste his skin, feel the roughness of his stubble against her lips. No matter how hard she tried, impossible to erase the memory of that sensation.

She'd been so glad to see the change in him. Another step away from bitterness and resentment into living. Her joy bubbled over into impulsive action.

Still, that didn't make the kiss any less a mistake. She hadn't missed the way he'd stiffened and pulled back from her, suggesting her touch wasn't welcome. And though Hope said nothing, the thunder of the cascade they neared rendering conversation impossible, Lainie hadn't missed the gleeful flash in the girl's bright eyes.

No doubt, the dutiful daughter and loving sister would report the kiss to Marlene, and they'd redouble their matchmaking efforts.

Exactly what she didn't need.

If only she'd prepared for this trip better. Gone back to Bethesda and worked till she earned more money to fund the tour. Then she could've opted for the three-day turnaround on the engine and been out of here in a week with no worries about blowing her budget.

She hadn't, and each day here, she stacked new mistakes atop old ones. Spending more time than necessary with Adam surely topped the list. Especially after Marlene's unintended reminder yesterday reinforced the need to keep her distance.

Deciding to stay longer to help Adam sounded good in theory. Just not if she behaved unprofessionally.

He *had* been her patient, and some would consider he still was, even though they'd both left the hospital. Time to start behaving that way.

Hope halted as the path veered far closer to the river. She touched

Lainie's sleeve and bent in close. "If you really want to get wet, you'll feel the spray just a step or two further on. But I warn you, it's cold! There's already been a snowfall higher up the mountain. I'm stopping here."

"I won't let myself get too wet," Lainie shouted over the vigorous roar. "And a little cold water won't hurt me."

She couldn't explain why she wanted to feel the spray. But doing it felt important.

After squeezing past Hope on the narrow trail between sweeping cedar boughs and waist-high ferns, probably lush and green in spring and summer but now browned and crisped by the chill, she stepped nearer the turbulent river. The trail opened up onto the falls, right where the water crashed onto an outcrop, breaking the smooth cascade.

And the noise — roaring, rushing, encompassing noise! — enveloped her. How could such sound produce such... *silence*? For suddenly, nothing else existed.

At last, the spray kissed her face and hands. Icy enough to make her shiver, but also real. Living water. Somehow, it thawed a numbness in her soul that froze her when Dad died, a numbness months on the road solidified.

Eyes closed, she spread her hands wide in wordless prayer, opening her heart and mind to God, the Creator of all this beauty. Time to let go of her fury over Dad's death. To start trusting He brought her here to Sweetapple Falls for a reason. To trust He brought her back into Adam's life for a reason.

To trust that if He really *could* turn all things to good, even our stupid human mistakes, maybe He could create something better from her unprofessional behavior, too.

Not that she intended to kiss Adam again. Making that mistake once was enough.

Just...maybe she could stop beating herself up for it. And stop beating herself up over her feelings.

CHAPTER ELEVEN

FOR ALL HE kidded himself he'd only come to church today to make Mom happy, Adam knew it was something more.

Someone, not something.

Lainie.

Mom had maneuvered them into sitting together. Then she and Hope excused themselves to sit with Petra. The oldest trick in the playbook.

Would God mind how he was far more aware of her presence — her lightest floral scent, her smallest move, her sweetest voice uplifting the worship songs — than any part of the service? Not the Bible readings. Not the prayers. Definitely not the sermon Pastor Dan enthused his way through now. He couldn't even say what Dan's topic was.

None of that mattered or even registered. God had different plans to reach him today, different ways to work in his life and get him to face all the things he'd resisted facing.

God used Lainie. His blessing sent directly by God, even if only till he got her bike roadworthy and waved her off to the remaining states on her list. She'd given him the wake-up call he needed.

At the karaoke, he'd asked for proof God still cared, proof everything *did* have a purpose. Even as he asked, the proof had been right up there on stage.

Being around Lainie again reminded him of the man he'd been.

The man he'd been in the hospital. Optimistic, faith-filled, God-trusting, sure it would all work out fine. Not the super-fit, gung-ho combat medic, carrying twice as much kit as his buddies and proud of it, but the core of him when all the rest was stripped away.

Focusing on all he'd lost, not all he still had, blinded him to the man he could be.

In his resentment over his losses, he'd blamed everyone else. The insurgents — for planting the IED. The doctor — for insisting on the amputation. The Army — for finding him permanently medically unfit, even for a desk-jockey job. Lainie — for disappearing and not being there when he needed her most. God — for letting it happen.

The one person he hadn't blamed for his losses was himself.

He'd blamed himself for living, sure. Raged at God, asking why he survived when his comrades all died and he'd been helpless to save them.

Survivor guilt. Most survivors got it, and he'd had it bad.

What he'd never let himself see was how his own choice of how to respond to all this wrecked his life just as badly as his injuries. Maybe more.

The blast didn't take away the man he'd been. The amputation didn't. The Army or Lainie didn't. God definitely didn't.

He'd thrown that man away. Him, Adam Trevor Davis. Every time he'd chosen resentment over faith, despair over hope, blame over responsibility for his life. The gift in Lainie's return wasn't enjoying her sweet presence for a couple of weeks or feeling more alive than he had for a year thanks to the exquisite ache of his longing for her. Wonderful though her being here was, her gift for him was something bigger. Something spiritual as well as emotional. Without meaning to, she forced him to recognize the cause of his biggest loss.

Himself.

Switching off Pastor Dan's animated voice completely, he prayed.

Thanking God for bringing Lainie here and showing him what he most needed.

Asking God to heal his resentment and blame. To change his focus from what he'd lost to what he had left. To give him the persistence and determination he'd need to do the hard work of rebuilding his weakened muscles of faith, hope, resilience, and grit, just like he'd worked hard rebuilding his weakened physical muscles.

And also asking for the heart-deep strength to love Lainie enough to let her go when she chose to leave.

The sooner he got her bike fixed, the sooner he'd lose her.

But this time, he wouldn't lose himself.

Working beside her gave him a reason to get up in the morning, something he'd lost along with his leg and his old life.

After she left, he'd find out the man he really could be. He'd let losing his leg turn him into a depressed and bitter loser in every area of his life. He wouldn't let losing Lainie when she rode off into the sunset like the white-hatted hero in an old Western put him back there.

She wasn't his to keep.

God had brought her back to show him this. And a whole lot more.

Since he'd opened his eyes to the truth, God wouldn't let him forget it. And God would give him the support, the strength, and the sense of purpose he needed.

If he needed a mentor to show him how not to waste any more of his life on bitterness and regret, he just needed to talk to Josh Tanner. Shifting enough to do it without being obvious, he glanced along the row behind them to the kid. Seated beside his parents, Josh perched at the end of the pew in his wheelchair, face alight with faith as he gazed at the pastor.

Josh knew better than anyone that survival was a gift and to make the most of every minute of it.

And Josh's mom, Anna, now joyfully married to Josh's dad, knew better than anyone the price of holding onto resentment.

Shifting sideways in his seat provided an added bonus. Watching the emotions play on Lainie's expressive face as she too focused on the sermon.

God blessed her with such beauty, inside and out. Yet she seemed so unaware of it.

After the service, came the ordeal he'd grudgingly endured with gritted teeth during his last two church visits. The fellowship time. Pastor Dan finished the service with his usual reminder about the value of fellowship, then invited everyone to stay, have coffee, and chat.

The first test of Adam's new resolve.

Before anyone came over to speak to them, Lainie turned, her smile warmer than summer sunshine. "Wow. I loved his sermon. He's such a lively speaker."

Adam chuckled. "He is. Everyone likes Pastor Dan, even the

renegades like me who haven't been here as often as he'd like." Should he admit he hadn't heard a word of the sermon? "God really spoke to me during it."

True enough. God had. Big time. The simple insight that no one but him could take responsibility for turning his life around was a game changer.

"I'm glad." Her too-brief touch on his arm and the joy in her gaze warmed him more than her smile had.

Then Petra's friend, the one in the bar with Tom, rushed over to hug her, and the moment shattered.

He let it go.

Lainie wasn't a security blanket to cling to.

The pastor stood beside him, a grin wreathing his homely ex-boxer's face. "It's wonderful to see you here today, Adam. I hope you'll come along next week, too. I've given Ms. Sullivan some time before we start to share her mission with us."

Mission. A good word for Lainie's dedication to honoring her parents' memory by completing the trip. And a good bribe to get him back two weeks in a row.

Instead of making an excuse, he nodded and returned Dan's smile. "Probably."

The pastor's twinkling eyes and glance toward Lainie showed he'd figured the reason for the unusually positive reply. He'd be half right.

"Time to rejoin the human race." That was the other half.

"Praise the Lord! An answer to many prayers sent up from this town. I guess that means we'll see you next week?"

Adam nodded. "And every week."

"Great news." Genuine delight boosted Dan's hearty grip as he pumped Adam's hand. Then he glanced down the aisle, and his expression changed to hint at a grimace. "Oh, shoot." Adam could swear the down-to-earth pastor restrained a stronger word. "I'm sorry, but we'll have to cut our conversation short."

Tabitha Whytecliff stormed up, her face thundery. "Pastor Dan! I'm shocked and disgusted. How could you provide such a bad example to the people in this town? I hear you were seen in the bar on Thursday night. The *bar*, of all places. Disgraceful! No wonder our Sunday school teachers have no idea how to behave correctly." Her voice rising with every word, indignation shook her wattled throat.

He felt for Dan. As a teen, he'd been on the receiving end of

Tabby's tirades, too. More than once. Her sharp tongue could make the bravest man quail.

Far from quailing, Dan smiled gently and took the older woman's arm. "Tabitha, why don't we go somewhere private to discuss this?"

She shook off his grip and planted her feet. "No, we will *not*. I will not be silenced and held back from publicly shaming you as you deserve! We'll discuss this right here. The whole congregation should be present when the sins of their pastor are exposed."

"As you wish." Far from raising his volume and tone to match her outrage, Dan's voice became even more quiet and mild. If the pastor wasn't standing right beside him, Adam doubted he would have heard Dan.

"I *do* wish." Tabitha almost spat the words. "I wish we had a pastor who espoused traditional moral values."

A sigh lifted Dan's chest. "I'm sorry you feel I don't. I truly have no wish to offend you. Like all of us, I've committed sins I regret and repent of, but I don't feel going into the bar was one of them. Remember, our Lord spent much of His time with publicans and sinners. He went where the people needed him most."

She said nothing, just pursed her lips, but her glare spoke for her.

"I'm grateful I was privileged to be in the Pony Express when God worked something powerfully spiritual." Dan spread his hands wide, his eyes glowing with a spiritual passion even Tabby had to see. "You may have noticed we have more worshipers here than usual? I'm sure that's a direct, God-given result of what happened in the bar on Thursday night, thanks to Lainie Sullivan."

A ripple of agreement spread through the congregation.

Shaking her head, Tabby huffed and stomped away. As she left the building, slamming the door behind her, the disapproving mutters began. Directed at Tabby, not the pastor.

"Let's not judge, but love and pray." Dan raised his strong voice to fill the room. "As we forgive, so we will be forgiven. As we love others, so we will be loved." Then he lowered his voice to continue their conversation as if the interruption hadn't happened. "As I was saying, Adam, I'm very glad you plan to join us here more often. It's good news."

Similar gladness lit the beaming approval Lainie turned to bless him with as Dan moved away. Their gazes met and held, and something soul-deep without need for words passed between them.

Keeping his eyes focused on her, he swallowed the boulder-sized lump filling his throat. Another test. Could he simply enjoy the sweet gift of this moment rather than anticipating the pain of losing her?

A hearty slap on his shoulder shook him, breaking whatever connected them. Lainie glanced past him to smile at whoever stood behind him, then swiveled back to Petra's friend.

Rusty. Finally he recalled her name.

He turned, too, to see who'd delivered that friendly thump.

Deek. The guy had either the best timing in the world or the worst. "I hear you plan to rejoin humanity at last. Good news. So, does it mean you'll join us at karaoke next week, too? Maybe even grace the Friday Night Lights with your presence? Or is only the church so honored? The guys have missed you, ya know."

Seemed his shift in thinking shifted Deek's awkwardness around him ever since he came home, too. Could be, his own attitude had been the awkward thing all along.

"Don't push it, bro," he warned. "From Grinch holed up in my cave to out there every day is more like an overdose of the human race."

His buddy rolled his eyes. "Funny, all the rest of us manage it."

"I don't know if you've noticed." Adam tapped his leg's hollow titanium stem above the knee.

Deek laughed. "Now that you mention it..."

They ribbed each other for a few more minutes with the relaxed camaraderie they'd had before the bomb blast.

"So, Friday Night Lights. Back to the land of the living means back to football, too." Deek didn't give up. "There's a demonstration game this week in Orchard Bridge. We're all going. The guys who are paired up are taking their girls along." He cast Lainie a glance loaded with significance. "You could ask Lainie."

Was everyone in this town determined to get him and Lainie together? Adam wanted that, too, but all the ham-handed matchmaking was far more likely to scare her off.

Thankfully, deep in conversation with Rusty, Lainie gave no sign of having heard Deek.

"Let's see how the week pans out." A safe, noncommittal answer, and Deek would have to be content with it. He wanted to make the most of his time with Lainie, sure, but if he said yes to every opportunity for time with her at group events, his joke with Deek about overdosing on human contact wouldn't be too far wrong.

For time with Lainie, it would be worth it, of course. But he hoped by Friday he could ask her for a real date, not a loud and busy group outing with his buddies.

After Deek, fielding everyone else came easier than the other two times he'd come to church. Not exactly easy, but easier. Even one or two of Tabby's equally sharp-tongued friends had a kind word for him.

The way to stop people pitying him was to stop pitying himself.

Then live a life no one *could* pity. With God's help, he'd learn to do that again. Make himself a man worthy of asking Lainie to come back to Sweetapple Falls.

And pray she said yes.

CHAPTER TWELVE

THE DAYS PASSED way too fast. Lainie had wondered how she'd fill the weeks of waiting in a small town. Instead — Thursday morning already.

After breakfast with Marlene and Hope, she retreated to her pretty guest room, piled the pillows up against the headboard as a backrest, and pulled out her Kindle. With its keyboard case, the tablet made a portable mini laptop. Good enough for most things she'd want a laptop for, once she found the right apps.

Time to catch up on her neglected journal. Time to look back on the week.

Hard to believe an entire week passed since she arrived. In some ways, it had flown. In other ways, it felt she'd lived here a lifetime.

In good ways.

Adam was wonderful. His family was wonderful. Sweetapple Falls was wonderful. And finally, she again believed God was wonderful, too.

Being in this town healed parts of her she hadn't known were broken.

Feeling at home, welcomed and accepted, helped. Feeling part of a family again, when she'd been isolated since Dad's death, helped. Having people with straightforward and heartfelt faith around helped, helped a lot. Seeing the change in Adam and knowing somehow she'd made a difference helped most of all.

It made a difference for her, too.

Seemed she really *did* need to be needed. Michael had been right.

Maybe she was looking for someone to rescue, rather than a healthy relationship.

But did that matter, when she'd be moving on? What mattered was Adam. The change in him.

Every day, she saw it more. The Adam she'd admired in the hospital. He didn't hide in his apartment, but came out and engaged with people again.

He'd chosen life. It showed in everything he did.

And she thanked God for it. If the only thing her stay here achieved was helping nudge Adam out of his hopelessness, it was so very worth it.

He radiated strength and determination. Genuine emotion sparked his eyes and voice. A welcome replacement for the despair deadening his eyes and drooping his shoulders, as she'd seen when she arrived and seen again in Josh's first YouTube interview.

He'd become more the Adam she'd known before, purpose-driven and positive. Yet better.

There, his faith was focused on the future. His certainty God would heal him and he'd rejoin his unit. When she'd arrived, he gave the sense of a man with no purpose, stuck in the past, held prisoner by loss and resentment. Now, she had the sense of a man grounded in the realities of his present life.

Maybe more so than she was, with all her focus on moving on.

No, not true. She could safely ignore that whisper. Wasn't her purpose completing the tour for Dad and Mom? She hadn't been able to stop either of them from dying, but she *could* fulfill their goals. Surely that was a worthwhile purpose. And one she couldn't allow anything to hold her back from.

Even Adam. No matter how much she loved seeing the man he was becoming.

Pushing that inner whisper away before it said more, she focused on cataloging her week.

At the falls on Saturday, he'd waited patiently at the lookout so she could explore with Hope. He'd even cracked jokes.

At church on Sunday, he'd told the pastor he'd decided to rejoin the world, and then he proved it. As he chatted easily with people in the fellowship time, no one seeing him would have guessed what he'd survived.

Monday, Adam drove her across town to the Tanner's big

Victorian. The clapboarded house, loaded with porches and turrets, gleamed with care and love. Like almost every building in Sweetapple Falls, it also boasted an impressive adornment of Christmas lights, ready for the official Christmas Lights festival on Saturday. Judging by the eye-popping color scheme, Anna and Luke let their son design the display.

She'd warmed to the family immediately from Anna's first words of introduction, rolling her eyes and chuckling. "Yes, Anna Tanner. I know. Proves how much I love my husband, right?"

She'd even warmed to Josh's black-and-white house pig, Patty Pork Pie, who sat in front of her like a dog, begging to be petted.

And she'd loved seeing the new Adam, inspiring and encouraging, shine out from his second interview with Josh. She couldn't claim credit for Adam's healing. God's healing touch made the real difference. That, and Josh's amazing example.

On Tuesday, her coffee afternoon with Rusty, Adam watched his niece and nephew after school while Marlene worked, so Petra could join them at the diner. Anna happened to be there delivering one of her wonderful paintings since the diner also served as an art gallery, so Petra called her over to join them.

The coffee was good, the huge slice of apple pie they shared delicious, and the conversation even better. If Lainie lived here, she'd be overjoyed to call these women her friends. Kindred spirits.

"The race that knows Joseph," Rusty said, quoting Anne of Green Gables.

When she and Petra returned to the house, they caught Adam, Marty, and Treeva playing a riotous game involving lots of shouting plus slamming their hands on the table. The kids clearly adored their uncle. Treeva even commented how good it was to have Uncle Adam back, as if he'd only just come home. In a way, maybe he had.

Adam clearly adored the kids right back. He'd make a fabulous father when he found the right wife.

No matter how she felt about him, she wasn't it.

Yesterday, Tom closed the Automotive for an extra hour over lunch and drove them on a tour of the Sweetapple Falls sights, in a huge classic Buick convertible his granddad had owned. She'd felt she should wave like Princess Di at the people who stopped to stare as they passed.

And this morning, since Hope didn't have any classes running,

Lainie planned to visit The Hope Chest, the quilting and crafting store Hope owned.

When she went downstairs, ready to follow Hope's simple instructions on how to get there, she found Adam waiting for her, seated at the dining table, crutches propped beside him. Impossible to ignore the leap her heart made at his smile.

Just joy over seeing her patient so much better. That's all. Totally all. Nothing more than that.

Sure it was. And wasn't that Patty Pork Pie flying past the window, too?

"Mind if I walk with you to Hope's?" Adam asked. "I need to push myself to walk further, and I want to use Hope's computer to do some stuff I can't do on my tablet. While she's giving you the grand tour, she won't be using it, and I won't be interrupting one of her lessons, either."

More time with him, given how she felt, might not be the wisest move. But how could she say no?

Especially when she didn't *want* to refuse.

Though she watched him carefully for any signs of needing rest, Adam chatted easily as he limped beside her to his sister's tiny store on Main Street, just past Maggie's diner. Wedged between two bigger, more historic buildings, the shape of the store suggested a narrow driveway, later closed in.

Hope had arranged the open-plan store into defined sections. The front part served as a gallery for local crafters, beautifully decorated in traditional country style for the holidays, using natural materials like burlap, popcorn, and pinecones. Jammed with goods, the middle zone sold quilt fabrics and crafting supplies. The back area, with a big worktable and chairs, served as Hope's teaching and workshop space. Photos displayed on the noticeboard showed a happy group working on wreaths. Rusty, Petra, Anna, and a few others Lainie recognized from church or from them making donations at the Automotive.

"If you'd been here a few weeks earlier, you could have come along," Hope explained the photos. "That was our Christmas wreath making day. We all had fun. If you look closely, you'll recognize some of the wreaths from front doors you've passed."

She did. Longing surprised Lainie. She'd never had time for this sort of homemaking stuff. Never really wanted to. Somehow, now she did.

While she admired the stunning handmade quilts and handcrafted products, took loads of photos, and listened as Hope explained the folk-art heritage behind quilting patterns and stitches with an enthusiast's delight in her craft, Adam waited without a murmur of complaint.

After asking Hope if he could use her laptop and print a few things, he'd sat at her worktable engrossed in whatever he had on the screen.

Though he hadn't focused on the computer *all* the time. Sensing his gaze, Lainie glanced across at him more than once. He didn't pretend he wasn't looking at her. Each time, he simply melted her with a slow easy smile, then returned to whatever he was doing.

Leaving Sweetapple Falls would tear something from her. Especially after another week or two becoming more embedded in Adam's family and hometown.

And of Adam becoming more deeply embedded in her heart.

Maybe she should pray her engine came back early.

As they prepared to depart Hope's store, his cellphone rang. The one-sided conversation told her she didn't need to pray for that anymore.

Disappointment ambushed her. No matter that staying longer would on intensify the pain of moving on. She didn't want to leave yet.

Adam ended the call, shaking his head. "That was Tom. Hard to believe this, but he says the engine is back at the shop. He wants us to go straight over, if that's okay with you both?"

"Sure," Hope said.

"Sure," Lainie echoed, struggling to gather her scattered thoughts. Impossible to guess if the engine's early return pleased or saddened him.

She didn't know what she should feel. Only what she *did* feel.

Dragging in a deep breath and straightening her shoulders, she arranged her expression into a pleasant smile. Or what she hoped would pass as one. "Wow. That's fast. If you want to check on the engine right away, fine."

Adam lifted a shoulder. "As long as it's a well-done rebuild, no harm in them getting it done fast. I guess they didn't have much else to work on."

Yes, there *was* harm, not that she could say so out loud. She wasn't ready for this.

Ready or not, the engine was back. No choice but to accept leaving earlier was meant to be. Something so unexpected had to be a God thing.

She turned to Hope. "Thanks for showing me the store. I love your quilts and the way you've decorated it."

Hope's lips wobbled. "I've loved having you here. Anytime. I'm just sorry you're leaving us so soon."

Me, too. Best not to utter her instant response. Instead, she hugged Hope. "We'll need a few days to get the bike together and ready to ride. Besides, who knows? Maybe I'll come back sometime and visit again."

Her attempt at cheer fooled no one. They all knew once she left, she wouldn't return.

After walking to Tom's workshop, Adam needed to sit in the office and rest, sipping on a soda, elbows propped on the desk for support. Probably to be expected. His weight training built strength, not endurance.

Concern still gnawed at her. Had he tried to do too much and set back his recovery? She did her best to assess him without being too obvious.

His twisted lips and raised eyebrow told her he'd noticed her surreptitious glances. "There's no problem, so don't worry. I haven't walked this far since getting my new best friend, that's all." He slapped his prosthetic leg. "I'll sleep sound tonight."

Impossible to restrain her doubtful glance.

Adam rolled his eyes. "We *do* need to check the engine. I'm not acting tough, pretending I feel no pain. I know my limits, and I haven't pushed past them. Anyway, I haven't tried to tell you I'm fine. That's when you need to worry."

That won a strained chuckle from her. "Okay." If she was keeping score, Adam won that point. Still, the single word emerged reluctantly. After seeing how well he'd played Mr. I-Feel-No-Pain in the hospital, she couldn't be quite so sure about his pain levels.

Scooting the office chair across the room, he stopped at the door and grinned back at her. "See? I'll humor you. My butt will stay in this chair. I'll even ask Tom to pry the crate open and hoist the engine out. Happy now?"

Not really, though his irresistible grin tugged her smile in response. But knowing how much he hated fuss, she wouldn't let herself fuss over him. Instead, she blew a raspberry to express her disbelief.

Silent laughter shaking him, he swiveled the chair, then zipped out the door.

Grinning broadly, Tom joined them beside the crate. "Surprised to have it back so fast?"

"Amazed, more like. Their website says up to three weeks." She eyed Tom, suspicion growing. His air of satisfaction. His complete lack of surprise. Something was up. "You're not nearly as surprised about it as us, are you?"

His smug grin widened. "Nope. I saw how upset you were about needing to stay three weeks. Your speech at the karaoke impressed me with how important your trip is. So I called the guys at J And M and paid the extra for the rush return. Didn't you wonder why I haven't made any other donation?"

That explained it. Unable to decide whether to hug Tom or smack him, she simply stared at him. "No. I didn't. Not at all. Letting us use the workshop was already a big donation. I'll give you another receipt for what you paid. It should count as a deductible."

"Okay, I'll accept that. At the time, it seemed the best thing I could do. Help you get back on the road faster to go on with your fundraising." He glanced from her to Adam, doubt clouding his expression.

"I'm very grateful, and it was hugely generous of you." With an effort, she forced a smile. She really should be far happier.

"Thanks, Tom." The dry edge to Adam's voice suggested he wasn't overjoyed, either.

The engine they winched from the crate appeared perfect. Shiny and immaculate as a brand-new motorcycle engine. Nothing hinting at its thirty-plus years.

After examining it carefully, Adam nodded. "Looks like they've done a good job." He handed her a printed sheet taped to the engine. "You need to follow this exactly, especially keeping the revs in the right range. Watch the oil pressure, too. The engine needs TLC till everything's bedded in."

She grimaced over the detailed instructions. "Hoo boy. The next few weeks will be interesting."

"I did warn you." He looked up from the engine. "We'll do all we can to get some miles on it before you leave. I don't want you on the road with an untested engine. The point of the rebuild is to ensure you don't run into any trouble out there."

Realizing the break-in process gave a good excuse to stay a little longer lifted her spirits far more than it should. The thought of leaving didn't sit comfortably.

At all.

A part of her had foolishly begun to hope. Hope Adam returned her feelings. Hope God would miraculously make it okay to see what developed between them.

But that wasn't an option. Time to remind herself of what she'd come dangerously close to forgetting.

She *had* to finish the ride. She was his nurse. He was her patient. And after Michael, she couldn't trust her feelings for Adam. Any more than she could trust what he might feel for her.

CHAPTER THIRTEEN

AMAZING HOW QUICKLY the bike went back together. Faster than it took to dismantle it.

Maybe faster than Lainie wanted.

By late afternoon, Adam had completed all the rebuilder's recommended initial actions, put the engine back in the bike, and reconnected everything. He lowered the height of the hoist so she could start the bike up for the first cautious test while he checked what needed checking.

Everything sounded right to her, but she held her breath till she saw him grin.

"The readings are exactly where they should be. It needs to cool down before we do more. Time to call it quits if you want to clean up and get to the karaoke. You're tonight's star, after all."

"I wouldn't say so." A snort escaped her. "I'm definitely not going to sing tonight, that's for sure. But I should be there the whole evening, I guess, since they're making it a fundraiser."

She didn't want to ask if he'd be in the bar again. He'd worked hard on the bike, and she shouldn't pressure him. Still, she silently hoped.

Next week, who knew where she'd be? Southern California? Maybe even New Mexico? Since she had what she'd thought she wanted, her bike ridable again, her few remaining days with Adam felt way too precious to waste.

Last Thursday, she'd worn jeans and a sweater to the bar, with her leather jacket for warmth on the way there and home. This week she dressed with more care. Not the extreme of borrowing a blingy frock, but now was the time to break out her one good dress. Even a pair of heels. Just low-ish ones, instead of sneakers or motorcycle boots. Hope loaned her a pretty coat, so she wouldn't need to wear her leather jacket.

The appreciation glowing in Adam's eyes when she walked into the living room sped her heart and trembled her all over.

She shouldn't feel so glad. Not really.

Not at *all*.

But still, she did. A deep womanly satisfaction warmed her to the core. His freshly pressed shirt and chinos suggested he'd tried harder tonight, too.

"Look at the pair of you!" Marlene's grin showed where Adam inherited his. "You both scrub up nice."

This looked too much like a date. Suddenly shy, Lainie rushed into speech. "Marlene, are you coming?"

"Not me. I have an early hospital shift tomorrow." Marlene brandished a bundle of new romance novels. "Besides, my subscription books arrived today. I have reading to do."

"What about Hope? She usually goes." Desperation ricocheted through her. If she and Adam went to the bar together, this didn't just look like a date.

It *was* a date.

Marlene waved them off cheerfully. "Not tonight. She's staying over in Orchard Grove with Noelle and Faith. It's just the two of you."

With an effort, Lainie kept her smile in place. Just what she didn't want.

But hadn't she told herself these last few days were too precious to waste? If her engine returning a whole two weeks early was part of God's plan, tonight had to be, too. Along with the football game tomorrow and the Christmas Trail on Saturday.

She didn't know why He'd want this. She didn't know how she'd get through it.

So many reasons for her discomfort.

And the main one? Even if tonight *was* a date, even if Adam *did* more than like her, trying to believe he might love her panicked her more than she could say or understand. The guff about professional ethics was only a defense. And an unconvincing one.

But just like with her engine, her only option now was to take a deep breath, trust God, and roll with it.

By Saturday evening, Adam admitted he was lost. Hopelessly, irretrievably, irrevocably lost in the type of love that didn't fade easy.

A woman like Lainie was hard to forget. Even harder to ignore.

Especially when she sat so close beside him, perched on a hay bale in the decorated wagon hauled by Bill Macpherson's Victorian steam tractor. The happy adults and excited kids crowding onto the charity ride around the Christmas Lights Trail pushed them together on the same bale. He didn't mind one bit, despite his soul-deep awareness of her and the discomfort of the tailgate pressing into his hip.

Lainie would soon leave. He accepted that. Her trip meant too much to her to ask her to stay. At least he'd have these sweet memories.

Throwing him a glance that spoke loud and clear — "Make the most of this opportunity" — Mom had shepherded Noelle, Faith, Petra, and the kids onto an earlier hayride, leaving him alone at the craft fair with Lainie. Though he'd had to sit it out as she toured each stall and stood chatting with Hope at her quilting booth, he'd had the pleasure of watching the woman he loved. He'd never tire of the changing expressions on her mobile face, the lilt of her voice, or the easy grace of her walk.

While Mom took care to keep his sisters away, God blessed him with the ideal setting. A star-bright cloudless evening, cold but not *too* cold. The beauty of the Christmas lights. The groups of carolers singing traditional songs, so much better than loudspeakers blaring. The mug of hot chocolate steaming in his hands. And Lainie, vital and warm, right here beside him.

He turned his head to drink in her beauty, storing the image as a snapshot in his mind. Honeyed hair waving on her shoulders, stirred a little by the breeze. Cheeks coloring rose pink, matching the cozy knitted hat and mittens she'd purchased at one of the stalls. Her face lit with wonder at the displays as each extravagantly light-decked home or store the tractor stopped at strove to outdo the last.

Just one thing marred her transparent delight — a hint of sorrow drooping the corners of her lips and shadowing her eyes.

"Dad would have loved this. Everywhere we lived, he always made a big deal of decorating our houses for the holidays." A sigh escaped her, barely audible over the noisy tractor.

Her first Christmas without her father. And if she insisted on leaving before Christmas as planned, she'd spend it alone. Wordless, he reached for her mittened hand and infused as much comfort and warmth as he could into the simple touch.

She let her hand rest in his, though she turned her head away. Blinking away tears? If only she'd realize grief wasn't something to be ashamed of. If only she'd let him kiss away her sadness.

He knew she had to leave. But everything this week convinced him not to let that be the end.

The kiss on his cheek at the falls.

The warm approval in her gaze when she'd caught him playing with Marty and Treeva like a kid.

The way she seemed to feel at home in Sweetapple Falls.

The date night at the karaoke. Though neither of them called it a date, it sure felt like one.

The way she fit right in with the guys and their girlfriends at the football game, cheering and laughing and eating hot dogs.

He wasn't the man he'd been a week ago. God had His mysterious reasons not to heal his physical wounds, but He'd healed the worse wounds on his mind and soul. Lainie's disabled fiancé had messed her around. With God's help, *he* wouldn't.

He just prayed she'd give him a chance to prove it, instead of running away.

As if sensing his gaze, she turned at last and met his eyes. A trace of tears still clung to her lashes. Awareness shimmered between them as real and solid as the hay bale they sat on, halting his breath in his throat. She said nothing, but her soft, slightly open lips and widening eyes suggested her breath hitched, too.

At the top of Mulberry Hill, the tractor stopped. No Christmas lights here, just a lone street lamp and a single park bench, giving a perfect view of the town lights. Dressed as they were for the wintery hayride, half an hour sitting here alone wouldn't chill them too much.

Thankfully, no one appeared to be at the lookout already.

Lord, please help me ask Lainie what I need to ask. Give me the words. Show me what to say and what to do.

Bill jumped from the tractor seat and ambled to drop the tailgate.

"Enjoy the view from your seats, ladies and gentlemen. Special request stop for Adam Davis and Lainie Sullivan. Everyone else, please stay on board for the rest of the ride."

His announcement, delivered in stern mock-officious tones like a bus driver, raised a laugh, and more than one knowing look cast their way.

Everyone stayed put. They'd have the place to themselves. Exactly as he'd hoped.

"It's another of my favorite places," he explained to Lainie. "You can see why." He spread his hands wide, taking in the view. And the words he left unsaid.

Because I need to talk to you alone. If I can't say what's in my heart in this romantic setting, I never will.

He eyed the distance to the ground and hesitated. One thing he'd left out of his plan. Only a couple of feet down, but it might as well be Everest.

When they'd boarded the wagon outside Maggie's diner, there'd been metal steps with handrails. Clearly designed for everyone to use, from eighty-something Mrs. Karlson to her nine-year-old great-granddaughter. No shame being seen hauling himself up, both hands on the rails.

But no steps or rails here. Only an audience.

Before his injuries, he would have simply jumped down. No problem, even in full kit.

Whether he'd get down without a face-plant now? Anyone's guess.

He had to try.

Perceptive nurse she was, alert for people's needs, Lainie stood, hopped out ahead of him, and moved to the same side as his missing leg. All before he'd fully pushed himself to standing. "Don't even *think* about doing this on your own. If you really intend to try, at least support yourself on my shoulder."

He'd better get this right. Or they'd both end up on the ground.

Bill glanced up at Adam, his tanned forehead furrowing. "Sorry. It didn't occur to me to figure how you'd get down. Why not stay for the rest of the ride, and I'll bring the steps along next go 'round?"

The sensible thing to do. But next time around, he might find a crowd already up here. Most folk knew this was the best place in town to view the lights.

"My job to think of it, not yours." Adam shook his head. "I'll try getting down this way."

"Sure. Your choice. If this is the side Adam needs support, how about we switch, Miss Lainie." Bill loosed a hearty guffaw. "I'm more than twice your weight."

No exaggeration.

A couple of passengers volunteered their help, but Bill waved them back. "No need. We'll do it."

Adam braced himself for the step down, praying his prosthetic knee would lock and hold him. If he misjudged, the burly farmer could probably pick him up. *After* he'd fallen flat on his face. He'd just have to suck up the humiliation.

What he wanted to say to Lainie was too important not to try. Keeping to the rules of his old life, priding himself in not needing help from anyone, wouldn't help him create a new life. It only created frustration. He'd been kidding himself to think otherwise.

Thankfully, he didn't need to put Bill's strength to the test.

By supporting his weight on the man's meaty shoulder and merely steadying himself on Lainie's slender one, he managed. After some awkward maneuvering, he stood on the ground beside Bill while Lainie reached into the wagon for his crutches.

"Thanks, Bill. I owe you."

The older man shrugged off his thanks. "All part of the service. I'll throw the steps in the wagon when I come around next."

Once Adam balanced securely on his crutches, the tractor trundled away, leaving him with Lainie. Though a car could pull up or walkers appear on the shortcut footpath between streets any moment, the first time they'd been truly alone all week. She glanced at him uncertainly, head tilted to one side.

Lord, please keep me from messing this up!

He pointed to the seat. "There's a bench we can sit on and a better view of town all lit up than anywhere else in Sweetapple Falls. May as well enjoy it. We have half an hour before Bill comes back."

The tractor's rumble faded, giving way to the whisper of wind through the leafless trees in the park behind them, the carols drifting up from the church hall where the Crafts-and-Cookies Fair was still in full swing, and the pounding beat of his heart.

CHAPTER FOURTEEN

ADAM CLEARED his throat and readied himself to speak. Despite his deliberate attempts to slow and even out his ragged breathing, his heart still raced faster than it ever had. Even when facing battle, he couldn't recall it accelerating like this.

"In spring, it's beautiful up here. The meadow behind us is thick with wildflowers, and the pears and cherries are in blossom."

"It's beautiful *now*." She nodded slowly. "I can see why you thought it worth trying that stunt to get down from the wagon. I wasn't sure you should."

Negotiating the uneven ground to the weathered timber seat took all his concentration. He waited till he'd lowered himself to sit and laid his crutches aside before replying. "I figure I need to take some risks to get what I want. Not trying to push myself beyond 'I'm fine' and 'I can manage' hasn't served me too well."

"Maybe they don't serve any of us too well. At least not *all* the time. Though I don't know if I'm ready to quit wearing the T-shirt yet." Her lips quirked to one side as her face creased. He waited to see if she'd say more, and finally, she exhaled. "So have you decided what you want?"

You. Way too soon for that.

"Some things, yes." He glanced at her, measuring how much to say. Talking about deep heart and soul stuff didn't come easy. "I've thought a lot this week. How I need to take responsibility for making what I want to happen in my life, well, happen. No one else is going to do it for me."

She sat beside him. Not quite as close as he'd like, but closer than she'd been. Her open, interested gaze invited him to say more.

"When the Army let me go, I had no idea what to do with myself. It felt like I'd died back in the transport, along with all my buddies. My old job gave me my only sense of purpose. Being 'Doc' Davis and doing all I could to stop guys dying in combat when they didn't need to. That was my life."

"I get that. Totally. For me, nursing gives me that purpose." Waving over her leather jacket and jeans, she shrugged. "Even dressed like this, my new uniform, I'm still always a nurse. I don't take it off with my scrubs. And for now, my purpose is finishing the tour and raising as much money as I can for Mom's fund. Keeping my promise to Dad, most of all."

He nodded, staying silent. Not what he wanted to hear, but what he'd expected.

"So tell me, what have you decided?" She leaned a little closer, and he caught a whiff of her delicate perfume. Like a field of spring flowers transplanted to this winter night.

"Since this happened" — he slapped the socket of his prosthetic leg — "it hadn't occurred to me to think about it. I'd hoped to be 'Doc' again. Let it be my only goal." He'd talked about his sureness God would heal him and get him back to active duty often enough in the hospital. She'd known what he meant. "On Sunday, for the first time, I asked God what He wanted me to do now because I didn't have a clue. Apart from knowing the Army isn't an option."

"I'm glad you're getting a sense of direction again." Approval warmed her voice.

"Me, too. But if I'd expected His answer to strike like a lightning bolt, I'd be disappointed. It's come to me in bits and pieces through the week. I think He expects me to be an encourager, to inspire people." He chuckled and rolled his eyes. "Yeah, I'm not so inspiring right now. That first interview I did with Josh is the opposite of inspirational. But God's challenged me to get my life together well enough so I *will* be."

Lainie clasped her hands together under her chin. "I'm sure you will."

"Seems the best way to show people what's possible with God's help isn't getting back to my old life, but living a new one, despite my injuries. I just need to look at a kid like Josh Tanner to see that." As he spoke, his certainty grew. This really *was* what God desired for him.

"And?" She grinned, eyebrows raised.

"The first thing is to find how I can ride my Buell again." His excitement bubbled out into animated words. "I checked with Connor, the local deputy, and with my rehab counselor about what I'd need to meet medical requirements to drive or ride. The Deputy's a stickler for the letter of the law. If he says I'd be street legal, I can be sure I will be."

She nodded, approval lighting her face.

"Probably with my balance problems, a sidecar will be the only way. I need three wheels, not two. And I'll have to make other mods, like a gear changer, a reverse gear, and a power stand like your dad fitted on the Goldwing. Once I've done all that and got my bike back on the road, I could start a business helping other amps get riding again."

Her beautiful smile widened. "That's a wonderful idea. I'm so pleased for you!" She rested a hand on his arm and beamed at him, radiant in the lamppost's golden glow.

Now or never.

He traced a finger along her jaw, his eyes seeking hers. The warmth reflected there encouraged him. With gentle hands on her shoulders, he drew her nearer, lowered his head, and kissed her. Wild sensation rioted in him at the touch of her lips on his. Even better than he'd hoped, warm and sweet and right.

Far from resisting, her lips softened beneath his, and she leaned into his embrace. The kiss deepened, speeding his heart still more and melting him completely.

Then both hands flattened on his chest, and she pushed herself away. He loosened his clasp and lowered his arms, though they ached to keep holding her. What looked like panic shadowed the wide eyes gazing into his.

"I shouldn't have let that happen." The words tumbled from her. "I'm sorry."

"I'm not. I've prayed for that kiss." He'd rushed her, pushed things too soon. But still, he couldn't regret what he'd done.

"No, I really *shouldn't* have kissed you back." Jumping up, she paced restlessly, then turned to face him. "When will the bike be ready? I need to get moving again."

Blowing out a long, low breath, he stared at her. Her words contradicted her actions. The way she'd kissed him as if she meant to. The way she'd been the one to pull him closer. The way she'd responded to his lips.

What was she running from?

Here it was, the test he'd known would come. Loving her enough to let her leave. He wouldn't lie to make her stay. All he could do was tell the truth.

"It's ready, now, I guess. As long as you take it easy and follow the run-in instructions."

The relief in her eyes warned him not to ask the question he longed to, but he asked anyway. Now might be his only chance.

"Noelle tells me there's a temporary vacancy for an RN at the Orchard Bridge Memorial. And Mom's loved having you as a houseguest. Would you consider staying longer? Not canceling the rest of your trip, of course. Just staying for the winter. Till the bike's run in and the risk of snow has passed."

"No!" The word burst from her like a gunshot. "I can't. I just can't. I have to finish my trip. If I leave now, I'll get far enough south to beat the snow." She uttered a hollow laugh. "Anyway, you don't need me now. My patient is well on the road to recovery. No need for a nurse."

His lips tightened. Every step he took toward rebuilding his life, Lainie took a step away from him.

"I'm not your patient anymore. Haven't been for a long time. It's over six months since you nursed me. Nearer a year. I know your trip means a lot to you, and I wouldn't try to keep you from finishing it. But you could come back when it's done." He dragged in another deep breath. Should he say more? Say the words he'd never spoken to another woman? "I love you. Really love you. I want to marry you."

There, he'd done it. His stomach quaked.

Lainie pressed her hands together and raised them to her lips, eyes troubled, brow furrowed. "No. You might think you do, but you can't. Not really. It's just a nurse/patient thing." Desperation to deny the truth tightened her voice.

"It's not just that." His jaw tensed. "I know what I feel. If I fell in love with all my nurses, there'd be what, one hundred? Two hundred?" Shaking his head, he spread his hands. "Why just you?"

Without an answer, she shrugged helplessly. "I don't know. But I do know this — once a patient, always a patient. At least, when it comes to anything other than a strictly professional relationship."

"Makes sense when you're still caring for someone. But it has to change eventually." What would convince her? "Half the nurses in Sweetapple Falls married patients. Mom did."

"Marlene nursed your dad thirty-five years ago. Professional standards have changed since then." She lifted her joined hands as if begging him to understand. "Please, accept this, Adam. Nothing can happen between us."

So stubborn in her determination to deny his love was real. Why couldn't she accept the truth? Frustration roughened his tone. "Tell me, how many other patients have you kissed like that?"

She recoiled as if he'd slapped her.

Eyes flashing, she lifted her head. "None. And that's why I have to go. If the bike is ready, I'll leave tomorrow after church." Holding her hands in front of her like stop signs, she gave him no chance to argue. "I'm sorry to leave you here, but Bill should be back any minute. I need to start packing my trailer."

Exactly as he'd feared, Lainie spun on her heel and marched along the footpath to the community hall.

Marching right out of his life. And powerless to follow, all he could do was let her go.

On Sunday, her final day in Sweetapple Falls, Lainie more than half expected Adam not to go to church with them. After rushing home the evening before to do her laundry and begin packing the trailer, she'd slept poorly. Wrestling with her decision to run away and praying it wouldn't plummet him back into depression brought her no nearer a sense of peace.

She *had* to leave. If she lost her professionalism and lost her purpose, then what would she have? He said he loved her, and for a crazy heart-pounding moment, she'd let herself hope he really did. Then common sense kicked in.

It couldn't be true. Just the usual gratitude for nursing care. And what she felt was born of caring for him when he was ill. You couldn't spend all those hours working so closely and intensively with someone without developing some feelings for them.

Neither of them were truly in love. It just felt that way.

She'd been thankful to have her professional excuses to hide behind. Nothing fake about them, either. Sixty percent of nurses would agree — no relationships with ex-patients, ever.

But just as a good nurse looked for the signs her patients were ready for discharge, she needed a sign he'd be okay once she was gone.

Dressed for worship, he thumped into the kitchen as she, Hope, and Marlene prepared to leave. Relief rocked her. The sign of his recovery she'd asked for, freeing her to leave without guilt she'd made things worse.

But regret? Nothing could stop her regret.

She smiled uncertainly. His bland return smile gave little clue to how he felt. But at least he was here.

Marlene rattled her car keys. "Perfect timing, son."

At the car, Lainie jumped in the back beside Hope. At the church, she ignored Marlene's attempts to seat them together. Instead, she wedged in at the aisle end of a pew beside Petra and Noelle. More convenient for when she needed to get up to speak.

That was her excuse, anyway.

Her talk went over well. Or at least, it seemed to. No one nodded off or looked around the room or stared into space. Not too obviously, anyway.

Since many of the congregation were in the bar that night she'd delivered an unplanned speech, she changed things up. Tried to make it as interesting as she could. Told her own story of what she'd learned staying at Dad's side through his cancer treatment and palliative care.

How being there as a relative on the receiving end of care taught her so much more about the needs of cancer patients and their friends and family than her years of nursing school and experience as an RN. How some nights when things were tough for Dad, she'd longed for someone to talk to. Someone who'd listen, without judging or giving advice.

With every word she said, her certainty grew. God called her to this. She was meant to be a nurse. Meant to do this trip. Meant to get the charity up and running. This was her purpose. The reason God created her. The good He could bring from Dad's death.

By the time she sat again, nothing could shake her. Not Adam. Not anyone or anything.

She was right to leave. And right not to come back.

CHAPTER FIFTEEN

MUCH AS LAINIE longed to leave right now with her sense of purpose strong, she had a couple more hours to get through yet. The sermon. The fellowship time. The goodbyes.

Echoing Adam's words yesterday, Pastor Dan preached about purpose.

"Another Sunday and another week closer to Christmas. The day we celebrate Jesus's birth as our newborn King. But what sort of King? As a baby, the wise men and Herod expected He'd become king in a worldly sense by snatching rulership from the current king. As an adult, those around Him expected the same.

"On Palm Sunday, when the people of Jerusalem welcomed Jesus into town, they expected Him to seize political power and rule the city. His disciples expected that, too. But God's purpose was way bigger and way more important than a mere earthly throne. God intended to bring His gift of salvation to all who choose to accept it."

Pretty sure she'd guess what came next, Lainie tensed, wishing she could block her ears.

She couldn't, and Dan continued his sermon. "The path to God's purpose led via the cross. Without our Lord's obedience to the Father's will, Christmas would be meaningless. There'd be no Christmas gift. Christmas is the beginning of the story, not the end. The star the wise men followed didn't just lead to a baby in a manger. It led to the cross. Jesus followed God's plan and God's purpose, not what those around Him expected Him to do. So today, I'd like to ask you to consider whose purpose you're following in your life. Is it

God's, your own, or someone else's?"

She knew the answer — God's. When she'd given Dad her promise, she'd felt so sure, so certain God wanted her on this mission. Adam shook that, but now she had her certainty again.

As if he'd heard her thoughts, the pastor smiled. "Don't be *too* sure you already know. Maybe your real purpose is something far greater or far different from what you imagine. Maybe you're settling for taking the city when God wants to give you the world. Ask Him to reveal *His* plan and purpose to you. Trust that, when He shows you His will, He'll also open the way for you to follow it, at the right time.

"The best choice will always be the most loving choice. Remember, when Jesus was asked which part of the law was most important, He replied 'Love the Lord your God with all your heart and with all your soul and with all your mind.' And 'Love your neighbor as yourself.' When in doubt, choose love. It might be two thousand years since He said that, but His commandment hasn't changed. It will never change."

Well, neither would her sense of purpose. She still felt sure. No need to ask again.

The fellowship after the service dragged on forever. Last week, she'd enjoyed the opportunity to get to know people. This week, though she should welcome the interested questions about the charity and her trip, she struggled to respond as enthusiastically as they deserved.

Now, while she felt so sure, she needed to get going.

If only Marlene would say it was time to leave. Give her an excuse to go. But Marlene lingered, enjoying chatting with friends. Adam showed no sign of hurry, laughing with the guys she'd met at the football game on Friday.

She should be glad. She should be happy to see he'd accepted her decision to leave.

Instead, irrational hurt over how quick he'd gotten over her stung like poison ivy. He couldn't really love her. She'd been right.

Well, she couldn't really love him, either.

She'd just have to make sure she got over him as fast, too.

Rusty breezed over to her, then enveloped her in a hug. "Something told me you needed a hug today. Great sermon, wasn't it? Really made me think. Sometimes when we believe we have life all figured out is exactly when we most need to let God change us."

"Uh-uh." Keeping her answer noncommittal seemed safest. God had already shaken up her life a few too many times. She really didn't want Him doing it again. "My bike is ready to go. I'm leaving this afternoon." The words blurted out without thought. Now, why had she said them?

"Ah." The teacher nodded knowingly. "No wonder I felt guided to give you a hug. A lot of people here are going to miss you." Her gaze darted to Adam.

No. Not him. He'd already started forgetting her. And he was right to.

A sigh she hadn't intended to release escaped her. "I'll miss people here, too."

She would. Far more than she intended to.

"Awwww." Rusty hugged her again. "You'd be welcomed back, anytime." Someone called to her from across the room. "I wish you weren't going so soon. I gotta dash. You take care, you hear? Friend me on Facebook, and we can message. Don't forget us."

"I won't." Truth. She already felt the pain of leaving, no matter that she knew it was right.

Lainie made sure not to tell anyone else she was riding out of town this afternoon. Best just to go. She hated goodbyes. There'd be plenty enough of those.

Finally, Marlene announced they were ready to leave. With gritted teeth, Lainie smiled and nodded. She'd been ready for half an hour.

Back at the house, Hope tearfully farewelled her with a hug before rushing off to a baby shower in Orchard Bridge, clutching another hand-stitched quilt. Glad there'd been good reason to cut it short, Lainie escaped to her room. She really *did* hate goodbyes. Especially with people she'd come to care for.

After changing her dress for jeans and a light sweater and shrugging into her leather jacket, she left the hostess gift she'd hidden in the bottom of her wardrobe out on the dresser for Adam's mom.

When she'd seen the quirky ceramic teapot on an artist's stall at the craft fair yesterday, the brightly colored item screamed Marlene. She'd paid for it quickly as soon as Marlene left on her hayride, and then tucked the gift-wrapped parcel in her tote.

Because the teapot didn't feel nearly enough, she'd also purchased an online subscription for an extra year of those romance books

Marlene loved and written the claim code inside a pretty card. Surely, a can't-go-wrong gift.

Taking a deep breath and straightening her shoulders, she made one final check to ensure she'd left nothing behind, picked up her tote, and walked from the room to face the inevitable farewells.

At least she had a good excuse to put off the final goodbyes for a little while.

Adam and Marlene waited in the kitchen.

Pulling the trailer keys from her pocket, Lainie jangled them and lifted her tote. "Apart from this, everything's packed in the trailer. I need to bring the bike over from the workshop, then hook it up."

Adam looked up from his seat at the table. "I've got the workshop keys to let you in. I gave the bike a quick check before church this morning. Nothing suggesting you shouldn't get straight on the road. Just stick to the break-in guidelines, and watch the revs and oil temperature. Especially when you're towing the trailer."

He spoke impersonally, as if she were simply a customer he'd done some mechanical work for. She could do the same.

Wasn't this what she wanted? The polite professional and distant relationship she should have stuck to all along. Since she had it, she missed the warmth between them.

"I appreciate you taking the time to check. Thank you." Her tight smile stayed just as meaningless as his. "I'll take it easy. And you don't need to come along with me. If Tom's there, I can manage fine."

"Tom won't be there. And I want to. I worked on the bike, so it's my responsibility to make sure it leaves the workshop in good condition." As if she were just another customer with a rush job. Pushing up from the table, he stood, and then reached for his crutches. Automatically, as she'd done so many times over the past twelve days, she passed them to him.

Unlike every other day, they walked to the workshop in near silence. Adam unlocked the main roller door, and she pushed it high enough to walk and ride under.

"I feel so impolite, not saying goodbye or thanking Tom properly. He gave me so much." When she'd made her impulsive decision to leave, it never occurred to her she wouldn't see the mechanic before she left. All her thoughts had been focused on Adam.

Adam shrugged. "He'll understand. You could email or phone

him tomorrow. He's in Eugene for the day, visiting his daughter."

"Tom has a child?" Surprise rocked Lainie. He'd seemed pretty much a single guy, especially when trying to impress Rusty in the bar.

"He's a part-time dad." Adam's lips twisted. "His wife left him for another man and took their little girl with her. He was badly cut up by it."

"I'm sorry." Showed how mistaken judging by appearances could be. "I'll email him tonight."

She watched Adam scoot around the bike on the office chair, giving it one final, thorough check. He looked up and nodded. "It's as ready to ride as it will ever be."

Biting her lip, she hesitated, then said what was in her mind. "Would you like to ride back to the house behind me?" She didn't quite manage to keep foolish hope from coloring her question. Another memory to store away carefully — his arms wrapped around her waist, his muscular body pressed against hers.

Just one more time…

Lips twisted to one side, Adam lifted an eyebrow. "That really wouldn't be wise, would it?"

No, of course, it wasn't wise. But she craved it anyway.

She shrugged. "Okay. I'll see you there."

"I'll stay here. As I've decided to modify the bike, I'll take the opportunity to check my own bike and think about what I need to change. Goodbye, Lainie. I hope your mission brings you the satisfaction you deserve. I'll be praying for you." He held out a hand, not to hold but for a businesslike shake. Even such impersonal contact unsettled her.

She could do this. She had to.

Years of practice in the hospital let her summon a cheerful smile. "It will. Thank you for all your help, Adam. I appreciate it. And I'm so glad to see how well you're doing."

He smiled, nodded, and then turned to the big Buell as if she'd already gone.

So she'd go. This was it, goodbye.

After starting the engine then releasing the center stand, she rode off, one eye on her rearview mirror. Adam didn't look up or wave. Rather than the pain she'd expected, she just felt numb. Deep-to-her-core numb.

Back at the house, she hitched the trailer, then went into the kitchen. One last stroke of Nosy's head and a gentle pull of his ears. One last quick cuddle with Oscar, who stalked off indignantly with a swishing tail when she put him down.

Now to deal with the final goodbye.

It was every bit as bad as she'd feared. Eyes bright with tears, Marlene hugged her. "I wish you weren't going. I wish you'd stay, at least till after Christmas. I hoped..." She trailed off, leaving it easy to fill in the blanks.

Tears still stinging her own eyes, Lainie took the road out of town and then turned south onto the highway. As if she needed to put as much space between herself and Adam as possible, she rode and rode and rode. Only a near miss with a deer stopped her from riding on after sunset. The wildlife became more active at dusk, and if she hit anything, it wouldn't end well for her or for the critter.

At the next cheap motel, she pulled over for the night. The limescale-caked shower permitted no more than a few inadequate drizzles of water to escape. The hard, plastic-covered mattress crackled whenever she moved.

Totally livin' the dream, baby.

Unable to sleep, she found Dan's sermon echoing in her brain, repeating the same questions over and over. Whose dream *was* she following? God's, her's, or someone else's?

The answer didn't feel nearly so clear-cut.

Lord, is this where You plan for me to be? Or did I take a wrong turn and miss the right road? Dan said to choose love. I thought I had. I loved my dad, and this is what I promised him. Your Word says to honor your father and mother. That's what I'm doing. Isn't it?

Her justifications sounded puny as the fears she couldn't escape began to dance.

Fear of falling for another differently-abled guy, who might only value her as a caregiver. Might want her for only what she could do to help him, not love her for herself.

Fear not just Michael, but *everyone* she'd loved wanted no more than that from her.

Fear if she stopped looking after people and stopped fundraising, no one would love or even like her anymore. *Any nurse would do.*

Little by little, the truth seeped into her heart. As a girl, she'd gotten love and approval for taking care of Mom. "Mommy's Little Nurse" everyone called her. Then, feeling she had nothing more to offer, she'd grown up and gone to nursing school. Kept doing the same.

She hadn't *chosen* love. She'd tried to *buy* love with nursing care. Reduced it to a transaction.

I'll look after you if you'll love me for it.

God didn't love that way. And it wasn't the love He intended for her, either.

But if Adam wasn't seeking someone to look after him — and she truly believed he wasn't — she couldn't imagine what she had to offer a man like him. Brave, determined, amazing. Truly inspirational once he'd chosen to embrace life.

The warmth in his eyes when he gazed at her suggested he thought she was equally amazing. The thought of opening her heart to him and then watching him discover the real Lainie was as flimsy and transparent as tissue paper chilled her soul-deep.

He hadn't been her patient for a long time. Long enough. She'd convinced herself he still was because it felt safer. Her professional standards became a shield.

Had she really left Adam because she'd chosen love? Or had she left love all those miles back in Sweetapple Falls, using her tour and her professionalism as excuses to avoid the risk of staying? The risk of being real with someone without her uniform to hide behind. The risk of loving like God did. The even scarier risk of letting somebody love her like God did.

Tears stung her eyes as she remembered all Jesus endured for us. Love without limits. A love so intense it terrified her. Yet He loved her like that. And He called her to risk loving the same way, too.

Loving Him. And loving Adam.

Only one way to find the love God planned for her.

Open her heart to Jesus and let Him in.

Really let Him in. All the way in. Accept Him as her Lord and savior in.

Not letting Him in just far enough to say "Sure, I'm a Christian, I pray sometimes and I go to church." That wasn't the sort of love He asked of her. The love He intended for her was altogether deeper, richer, more complicated.

Then tomorrow, she'd get up at dawn, turn the bike around, and go back to Sweetapple Falls. And pray she hadn't lost any chance of Adam's love when she chose the charity tour and her professional identity instead of him.

Adam had needed to choose life.

Now she knew she faced a choice, too. She needed to choose love.

CHAPTER SIXTEEN

LAINIE STOOD outside Adam's front door, praying he'd be in. Riding into Sweetapple Falls again felt like coming home. But as she waited for him to answer, the butterflies dancing in her stomach grew teeth and gnawed at her.

She'd parked her bike in the driveway and hurried straight to his apartment rather than going to the main house. Marlene would have welcomed her, for sure, but adrenaline pounded her pulse rate too fast to manage small talk or explanations. Shaking at the thought of spilling her heart to Adam, she gripped the railing.

Rising before dawn after a fitful sleep and riding for hours on two cups of coffee left her keyed up and jittery. Once she no longer hid behind excuses, the fears she couldn't avoid attacked her.

Since leaving the motel, she'd spoken to no one. Until she talked to Adam, her mind held words only for him. And for God.

Please, Lord, let him be home. Help me be honest with him and share my fears instead of pretending. Help me to trust You brought me back for a reason. And please please please don't let it be too late.

What if the way she'd clung to her professional ethics and the promise she made Dad, using them like force fields to push away the truth in her heart, had hurt him past the ability to forgive? He'd been so distant when she left yesterday.

What if she'd read too much into his kiss and his words at the lookout, fooled herself it meant as much as she hoped?

What if —?

Adam opened the door. Her adrenaline spiked higher, and she

clutched at the railing to stop wobbling.

"Hello, Adam." The soft, hesitant words trembled in the air between them.

He didn't answer. Just stared, a muscle in his jaw twitching, forehead furrowing, eyes disbelieving.

His T-shirt and shorts plus a light sheen of sweat suggested she'd interrupted his workout. For the first time, she saw his leg, without jeans or chinos covering his prosthesis. Her gaze dropped to the stump ending mid-thigh. The nurse in her approved how well it had healed. The woman in her restrained a gasp as an iron fist clenched her heart and squeezed.

More than ever, she admired Adam for his choice to leave despair behind.

Insecurity shook her as he stayed silent. She shouldn't have assumed he'd be happy she came back. Maybe her mistake hadn't been leaving, but returning. "I... I wanted to talk to you. But I can go if you'd rather not see me again." Disappointment choked her.

"Don't go." A wild sweet joy lit his face, setting hope blossoming in her chest. "I want you here. But I thought I was hallucinating. Imagined I'd heard your bike."

Thank You! Thank You!

"The bike's outside. And I'm really here." She clasped her trembling hands in front of her chest. "I...I need to tell you some stuff I should have talked to you about on Saturday."

"Come in?" As he swung the door wide, he sounded as unsure as she felt.

A compact but well-equipped kitchen filled one corner of the living room he led her into. Tidy, but not neatnik tidy. The closed doors likely hid his bedroom and bathroom. This room held simple furniture, chosen to suit the smaller space and a single occupant. The loveseat he waved her to would be cozy for two.

Not that she minded cozy. But instead of sitting beside her, he used one crutch to hook a chair out from the dining table. Awkward. At risk of unbalancing.

But somehow, she restrained her usual urge to jump up and help.

"Can I get you a coffee?"

The last thing she needed was more caffeine speeding the racing nerves already drying her mouth. "Could I have a glass of water, please?" Then she thought about it. With both hands occupied with his crutches, he'd have trouble carrying it. She moved to stand. "I can fetch it myself if that's easier? I shouldn't expect you to wait on me."

"But I want to. Sit down." Waving a crutch at her, he grinned, a hint of mischief in his eyes. That adorable grin she loved. "I'm fine. I can manage."

She rolled her eyes at his catchphrases. Once, she would've felt rebuffed by him refusing her help. Now she recognized she had to accept his need for independence. It was as much a part of him as his grin. "This I gotta see."

The teasing lifted her anxiety. Maybe everything would be okay.

"O ye of little faith. I have not one but *two* strategies for this." A few steps carried him to the refrigerator, and he held up out a pint-sized bottle of soda. "This is for me, to show strategy one. Make sure I wear clothes with pockets." The bottle wedged into the roomy pocket of his cargo shorts. "And two..."

After pouring a glass of iced water, he hooked a small round tray suspended on four cords to a support clipped to his crutch. The water didn't spill as the dangling tray balanced itself with his movements. He stopped in front of her so she could lift the glass. "Works great as long as I don't overfill things."

"Thank you." She swallowed a grateful gulp. "Clever. I should have guessed you'd have workarounds for everything."

Stowing his crutches in two slots attached to the table, he sat at the table and shrugged. "Not quite everything yet, but I'm working on it. The tray was Mom's idea. Because she works in eldercare, she knows about a lot of little things her patients find useful."

So much to learn. She welcomed the challenge. Healthy to admit she didn't know it all. "I've mostly worked in acute care, so I'm not up to speed on the rehab stuff. I wish I knew more about it."

Regret tightened his lips. "Me, too. I pushed to leave rehab too soon. Wasted too long refusing to adapt, struggling against things with simple solutions. As if shutting my eyes to problems and saying 'I'm fine' would make them go away. I still want to do all I can for myself, but I've no need to do it the hard way. It's only the past week or so finally I saw sense."

Since she'd been here? He'd hinted as much on Saturday. Gladness she'd been able to make a difference to him lifted her. God willing, they could both make a lot more difference to each other's lives.

He already had in hers.

"You're a week ahead of me. Maybe more. I only saw sense yesterday." Her cheeks heated, and she fought back an urge to duck her head. "I'm sorry I went away. *Ran* away, really."

"You came back. That's the main thing. Want to talk about it? I'm here, ready to listen." He spread his hands wide, expression open and accepting.

Adam knew how to listen. Another thing she loved about him.

Exposing the vulnerabilities she hid behind her nursing scrubs wouldn't come easy. But she had to try. Even though she barely understood some of this stuff herself yet. She gulped another mouthful of water, hoping it might melt the tightness in her throat.

"I realized how terrified I am of letting anyone get close enough to really see me. I *have* to do things to look after people because I'm scared, if I don't, people won't love me or even like me. It's just what I've always done." Surrendering a sigh, she shifted in her seat. "Mom was sick pretty much the whole time I was growing up. As a kid, I looked after her. And everyone told me how wonderful I was. When I was just playing with my Barbies or having fun with my friends, no one noticed me."

Adam nodded slowly, brow creased. "I've never thought it through like you have, but I guess I was the same about being 'Doc'. Helping the other guys made me feel stronger." He stopped to take a swig of his soda. "Explains why I took the honorable discharge so hard. I could have handled losing my leg if they'd let me keep my job."

How she loved his honesty and openness. A man in a million. "I'm glad you understand. But sorry you had to find out the hard way."

He shrugged. "I'll live. For a while there, I wasn't doing too well. I'm through the worst now. But you know, you're good at looking after people. You were the best nurse I met, in the hospital or in rehab. I always got the feeling you really did care." Sincerity echoed in his voice and softened his features.

"Thank you. I tried hard to be a good nurse." His praise warmed her, but her reaction was part of the problem. "But maybe I tried too hard, made it a compulsion. You've seen how I struggle to let anyone do things for themselves if I can help them."

"I could have noticed once or twice." He chuckled. "Don't worry.

I'll forgive you."

"I may need to remind you of that. I can't promise I won't still do that now and then. But I'll try not to." She prayed she wasn't assuming wrong. That sounded as if he thought they had a future together. And she liked the sound of it. A lot.

"I'll survive. I might even get to enjoy being fussed over."

"I hope so. Because it's still something I *like* to do, even if I don't feel I *have* to do it. Since God showed me the unhealthy side of it, I can let that go. I won't need to give care so much. That need in me made me ready to believe Michael loved me and I loved him. Really, he needed someone, and I needed to be needed. I wouldn't make the same mistake now."

Adam's face darkened. "My opinion of the guy hasn't changed. You know *I'm* not like that, I hope."

"I do. No one, who values their independence as much as you, could possibly be." She laughed, shaking her head. "In my opinion, you're too far the opposite."

"Good. I'd rather that."

"But till I saw my own unhealthy patterns, your independence bothered me. It might still exasperate me at times, but this was something far deeper. I knew you didn't need me, so I ran. You said you loved me, but I couldn't let myself believe it." Her clasped hands rose to cover her mouth, and she bowed her head, asking for the courage to say what was in her heart. "And because of that, I couldn't admit to how I felt about you, either."

"And how *do* you feel about me?" Hope lurked in his tentative smile. He wasn't taking her love for granted.

Drawing a deep breath, she met his intent gaze. "What I feel for you is so different from what I felt for Michael. It took real love to show me the fake. I love you."

No need to say more as delight sparked his eyes and he grinned the biggest, widest grin she'd ever seen. Picking up his crutches, he stood. Not to leave her, but to move toward her. He sat beside her on the loveseat, then reached for her hands. At his touch, a rush of sweet emotion washed over her.

Grin fading, his expression became serious. "I love you, too. I'll always love you. I don't want to rush things, but I want you to know I hope to marry you. If you'll have me, that is?"

His humility tore at her heart. She smiled, pouring all the love she felt for him into it. "I'd be honored to marry you."

Releasing his grip on her hands, his fingers cradled her face, tracing the curves of her cheeks, brushing softly over her lips. He gazed into her eyes as if she was the most precious thing in the world. Already close on the snug seat, his movement brought him even nearer. Her breath stuttered.

His head lowered, brushing tiny butterfly caresses on her cheeks, forehead, closed eyelids. At last, his lips moved to hers, in a gentle tender kiss like a pledge of love. If she'd held onto any doubts, his kiss swept them away.

She reached her arms around him to flatten against his strong back, drawing him even closer as her lips parted beneath his and the kiss deepened, lengthened, intensified, in a joyous union she'd never imagined existed.

Finally, Adam pulled back, breathing hard, eyes unfocused. "We should go to the main house right away. Mom will be there. Not wise to stay here alone." Emotion hoarsened his voice. "And I've changed my mind about rushing you. Let's get married as soon as we can. Right after Christmas."

Heart filled to overflowing, she smiled, thanking God for all His gifts. Especially, for the undeserved blessing of being loved by this wonderful man. "Sounds like a great idea.

EPILOGUE

IN THE BACK SEAT of Tom's Buick, Adam gazed at his bride, more beautiful than ever in white silk and lace, a fake fur jacket covering her arms and shoulders, a rug tucked around their legs keeping them warm despite the January chill.

Already bucking tradition with such a short engagement, they'd agreed to travel to the church and walk down the aisle arm-in-arm instead of separately. Lainie missed her dad enough without the who-gives-this-woman part rubbing it in. And he planned to start their marriage as he intended to continue it.

Together.

Staring into her beautiful eyes, he caressed the back of her hand with his thumb, as it nestled into his clasp. "I'll never stop thanking God for you and the way He's blessed our lives."

Lainie nodded, her lovely smile fountaining joy through his heart. "I thank Him for you, too. And for all He's done for us both. I needed His healing touch just as much as you did. He is so good. So many blessings."

Certainly blessings he'd never expected or imagined he deserved. But God had given him so much more than he imagined.

Just one month since he'd proposed, and so much had changed already. Today marked the beginning of a whole new life for them both.

Mom confessed she'd secretly arranged a collection, and the town contributed enough to pay the cost of his bike conversion. He'd let Josh apply for a grant, not for his own bike repairs, but to help him assist other disabled riders get back on the road again, instead. Lainie never mentioned it, but he knew she still hoped to finish her tour and raise more funds to support her mom's charity.

So once his bike was ready to ride again and winter had passed, they'd journey together as a delayed honeymoon.

He'd wanted to inspire others with what was possible, and the trip was just the way to do it.

As if driving them to church in this amazing car wasn't enough, Tom offered the use of an old unused workshop at the Automotive for as long as they wanted as his wedding present. Thanks to the generous gift from the town covering the bike modifications, Adam could spend the money he'd set aside for that on tooling up the workshop instead. Everything he needed to start his business would be here waiting when they finished the tour.

He gently squeezed Lainie's warm hand and slipped his other arm around her, drawing her near. "I didn't think I'd ever be able to say this, but I can see the good God has brought from my injuries. I'm more of a whole man now than when I was able-bodied."

"I'm so glad. You're all the man I'll ever want." Pulling her hand from his, she cupped his face and leaned in to kiss him, long and soft and sweet. Her tender yielding lips and the way she leaned into him promised so much more, once they were married.

The car stopped moving, and Tom's guffaw interrupted them. "Hey, stop that, you two! You're supposed to wait till Pastor Dan says 'You can now kiss the bride.'"

Adam winked. "I think he'll forgive us for getting a head start on the kissing part."

"I have this all on film, you know!" Josh chimed in from outside the church doors. He'd appointed himself chief videographer, with no objections from anyone.

"Film away, kid. Here's some more for you to catch on camera." Unashamedly in love with his bride, Adam held her close and kissed her again.

God was good. God was very good.

And since Lainie arrived in Sweetapple Falls, so was life.

THE END

THANK YOU FOR READING

I hope you enjoyed reading His Healing Touch! Thank you for spending this time with my story. I pray that you feel God's love, mercy, and grace richly blessing your life!

If you liked this story, you'll probably also enjoy my other books. There's the *Love in Store* series set mainly in London; *The Macleans* series, set mostly in Edinburgh; *Huckleberry Lake*, set in Idaho; and many other books to come. All include love, faith, characters overcoming real issues, and always, always ALWAYS, a happy ever after!

You can see all my currently released books on my website books page: www.FaithHopeandHeartwarming.com

Also, if you enjoyed this book, please consider telling other readers and posting a short review on Amazon, Goodreads, or anywhere else readers discuss books. Recommendations from happy readers are so very appreciated by authors, and it helps readers find books they like. Your opinion counts!

Blessings, and happy reading!

Autumn

BIBLE VERSES & OTHER REFERENCES

<u>Chapter 4</u>

Jeremiah 29:11 NIV

For I know the plans I have for you," declares the Lord, "plans to prosper you and not to harm you, plans to give you hope and a future.

<u>Chapter 8</u>

Matthew 18:20

For when two or three gather in my name, there am I with them.

Amazing grace! How sweet the sound
That saved a wretch like me!
I once was lost, but now am found;
Was blind, but now I see.

'Twas grace that taught my heart to fear,
And grace my fears relieved;
How precious did that grace appear
The hour I first believed.

Through many dangers, toils and snares,
I have already come;
'Tis grace hath brought me safe thus far,
And grace will lead me home.

The Lord has promised good to me,
His Word my hope secures;
He will my Shield and Portion be,
As long as life endures.

Yea, when this flesh and heart shall fail,
And mortal life shall cease,

I shall possess, within the veil,
A life of joy and peace.

The earth shall soon dissolve like snow,
The sun forbear to shine;
But God, who called me here below,
Will be forever mine.

When we've been there ten thousand years,
Bright shining as the sun,
We've no less days to sing God's praise
Than when we'd first begun.

(words by John Newton, 1779)

Chapter 15

Matthew 2:1-12 NIV

After Jesus was born in Bethlehem in Judea, during the time of King Herod, Magi from the east came to Jerusalem and asked, "Where is the one who has been born king of the Jews? We saw his star when it rose and have come to worship him."

When King Herod heard this he was disturbed, and all Jerusalem with him. When he had called together all the people's chief priests and teachers of the law, he asked them where the Messiah was to be born. "In Bethlehem in Judea," they replied, "for this is what the prophet has written:

"'But you, Bethlehem, in the land of Judah,

are by no means least among the rulers of Judah;

for out of you will come a ruler

who will shepherd my people Israel.'"

Then Herod called the Magi secretly and found out from them the exact time the star had appeared. He sent them to Bethlehem and said, "Go and search carefully for the child. As soon as you find him, report to me, so that I too may go and worship him."

After they had heard the king, they went on their way, and the star they had seen when it rose went ahead of them until it stopped over the place where the child was. When they saw the star, they were overjoyed. On coming to the house, they saw the child with his mother Mary, and they bowed down and worshiped him. Then they opened their treasures and presented him with gifts of gold, frankincense and myrrh. And having been warned in a dream not to go back to Herod, they returned to their country by another route.

John 12:12-13

The next day the great crowd that had come for the festival heard that Jesus was on his way to Jerusalem. They took palm branches and went out to meet him, shouting,

"Hosanna!"
"Blessed is he who comes in the name of the Lord!"
"Blessed is the king of Israel!"

Matthew 22:37-40 NIV

Jesus replied: "'Love the Lord your God with all your heart and with all your soul and with all your mind.' This is the first and greatest commandment. And the second is like it: 'Love your neighbor as yourself.' All the Law and the Prophets hang on these two commandments."

Chapter 15

Ephesians 5:1-2

Follow God's example, therefore, as dearly loved children and walk in the way of love, just as Christ loved us and gave himself up for us as a fragrant offering and sacrifice to God.

ACKNOWLEDGEMENTS TO

My superb editor, Dee at Brilliant Cut Editing, who really went above and beyond for me to get the first version of this story edited in time. Any errors in the text are all my own! She is just awesome, as well as being a beautiful demonstration of love and faith in how she lives her life. I truly could not have a better editor.

My writing buddy and dear friend Shannon Marie, for always seeing just where my stories need more work, and often coming up with exactly the right line to express what I struggled to say. She is a total blessing to me!

Paula Marie for her support, encouragement, and ramen noodles.

Logan's Mom for letting me use his T-shirt slogan.

My beloved husband Arthur, for his patience and love. Especially when I need to stay up all night to meet a deadline, skip meals, and say "Don't interrupt me, I'm writing," a dozen times a day!

As always, my deepest most heartfelt thanksgiving and praise to God for His love and goodness. No matter what happens in my life, I've learned to trust in Him. He's managed to bring good from my biggest mistakes and my worst disasters.

And thanks to you, dear reader, for coming this far with me. I hope this story blessed and uplifted you.

Stay up to date with my new releases as well as special subscriber-only freebies and special offers, by signing up for my mailing list. Sign-up links can be found at my website www.autumnmacarthur.com or by scanning the QR code.

Made in the USA
Columbia, SC
10 July 2024

38421405R00079